D0630619

THE
TWOFOLD
VIBRATION

THE TWOFOLD VIBRATION

Raymond Federman

Indiana University Press
BLOOMINGTON

The Harvester Press
BRIGHTON

Published jointly by

Indiana University Press   The Harvester Press Ltd.

Tenth and Morton Streets   16 Ship Street
Bloomington, Indiana, U.S.A.   Brighton, Sussex, England

Manufactured in the United States of America

Library of Congress Cataloging in Publication Data

Federman, Raymond.
  The twofold vibration.

  I. Title.
PS3556.E25T8   813'.54   81-47831
ISBN 0-253-18989-6 (Indiana)   AACR2
ISBN 0-7108-0460-1 (Harvester)

for Simone

But the persistence of the twofold vibration suggests that in this old abode all is not yet quite for the best.

SAMUEL BECKETT

Something that never changes with the night or the day, as long as the past represents the future, towards which it will advance in a straight line, but which, at the end, has closed in on itself into a circle.

JEAN-LUC GODARD

THE
TWOFOLD
VIBRATION

I

Hey you guys wake up, wake up, it's starting all over again, but this time it's going to be serious, the real story, no more evasions, procrastinations, and you won't believe this, it begins in the future, no I'm not kidding, well the near future, can't stray too far from the present, and besides there is a certain logic to keep in mind, a certain urgency too

what do you mean science-fiction, not at all, it's not because one wanders into the future that

call it exploratory or better yet extemporaneous fiction, that's right, a question of more space, room to expand forward and backward, a matter of distanciation if you wish, room to turn imagination loose on the spot and shift perspectives unexpectedly, sounds interesting, damn right, but no futuristic crap, I mean pseudoscientific bullshit, space warfare, fake theories of probabilities, unsolvable equations, strange creatures from other planets, ludicrous busybodies with pointed ears, wings instead of arms or wheels instead of legs, none of that, a way to look at the self, at humanity, from a potential point of view, premembering the future rather than remembering the past, but no gadgetry, no crass emotionless robots that crush the shit out of you when you don't submit to their notion of life, bloodless robots that take over your basic human functions, no none of that infantilism, at least within reason, no invasions of earth by superbrains, spaceship battles in the galaxies, worlds that collide, nothing spuriously progressive or regressive in this story, nothing prophetic or moralistic either, quasi-moralistic in the sense that things will get worse in the future if we don't stop messing around with ecology or the natural order of things, no, just a simple moving story

it begins in the year 2000, or just before, the story, the night before to be exact, new year's eve, December 31, 1999

the first sentence goes like this, If the night passes quietly tomorrow he will have reached the 21st century and be on his way, nothing extraordinary about that, nothing earthshaking, but I rather like that sentence, and besides don't you think it's a better beginning than Once upon a time there will be

it came to me during a sleepless night, and I have many of these lately with the way things are going in my mental stratosphere, no not stratosplit, stratosphere, just an image, it's not often that such a perfect sentence comes to one's mind, that's why I decided to exploit it, explore it as far as I could, to the outer limits of imagination, but of course within the possibilities of language, and it goes on telling the story of this guy, an old fart 82 years old now who is being deported to the colonies

the what, you ask, the colonies, the space colonies, be patient, everything will be explained, clarified eventually

which means that the old man was born in 1918, like my father, coincidentally, or for that matter like me, fictitiously speaking, what's the difference, we are all extensions of one another, the living as well as the dead, we all overlap within the twofold vibration of history, 1918 then, even though it is purely aleatory, you understand, dammit, doesn't take much calculation to arrive at that date of birth from the year 2000 if one retraces one's steps mentally into time and into history, though it's true, one can never be sure, he might be older than that, or younger, for all I know, he always looked ageless as for the space colonies, they are conquered planets, moons, satellites in the solar system, and even beyond, in the galaxy, the Milky Way, which were explored and civilized during the last part of the 20th century, and where

of course I have to invent the future, all right the near future only, move about among new forms, new concepts, project ourselves into the potential cosmological layout, but obliquely, at random if you prefer, and somewhat gropingly, I admit, a matter of precalling history

and where, we were saying, undesirables are sent, you know criminals and perverts, madmen or those who are considered physically or mentally abnormal, social derelicts, the useless ones, the good-for-nothings, and others too, isn't it a tremendous idea, old folks and sick people are also sent there, the incurables, that solves the problem of the aged, social security and medicare, and it also wipes out crime and unemployment, not to mention sexual perversion

artists too are sent there, yes especially experimental artists whose work is found totally unredeemable according to the new idealistic social and aesthetic norms now in vogue

but these annual mass deportations, always scheduled on new year's eve, have one advantage, they make more room for the rest of humanity, especially at a time when the world is quite overpopulated, but it's a good world, things are going well, relatively well, in that old world of ours, from a political, social, ethnic, and psychological point of view, that much must be said for it, peace all over, no more wars, no more revolutions and civil uprisings, no more terrorism, shit things are going well, no more aggressive politics, moral oppression, territorial occupation, all that disappeared just like that, pssitt, in a sudden stroke of worldwide peacefulness and fraternalism, sentiments which in the past used to be as foreign to us as to cockroaches

the possibility of improvement was in the air for a while you know, particularly with the drastic and still unexplained changes in weather patterns that occurred during the last two decades of the 20th century when the westerlies altered their course unexpectedly, yes for the better, right after the catastrophic winter of 1977, one of the coldest and most brutal winters ever recorded in human history, so bad, so disgusting, so infuriating, in North America especially, where the old guy was living at the time, Freezing my ass off, that many thought the earth had entered another ice age, but instead perennial warm air currents shifted direction and a much more temperate climate now extends as far north as the 60° latitude, well that does it for the weather

consequently no more food crisis, no more energy crisis, economic crisis, and related crises, how easy it is to solve human problems when you're writing an extemporary rather than a realistic story, natural resources are plentiful, as we knew they would be someday, and carefully used, intelligently exploited and distributed, and whatever is in short supply in this new era of agricultural and industrial abundance is imported from other planets

goodwill among men, and yes of course among women too, that goes without saying, and even among domestic animals, reigns all over, liberty, equality, fraternity, no not sorority, stop kidding around you guys, this is serious, are no longer empty words but terms that apply to everyone, and there is fair and just distribution of wealth among all the citizens of the world without the least discrimination or corruption, sounds fantastic, you're damn right, it's all decided, calculated, regulated, adjusted in advance by a gigantic humanized computer, I call it Onselacouledouce so we can have an easy term to refer to this friendly machine

okay, agreed, it was predictable, already as far back as the '50s, that computers would someday handle all human affairs, I do not pretend to be some kind of omnipotent seer, nonetheless everything now is based on scientific reasoning, scientific fair play even, and technological ingenuity I might add

I don't go much into the details of how that system, superb utopic system as some people call it, was established, but it works, believe me, it works, nor do I explain how the planets, moons, and other such once distant places were first explored, conquered, rendered livable, civilized, and subsequently turned into colonies, oh that's too bad you say because it might weaken the scientific premise of our story, not at all, that's left to the imagination of those who read, or will eventually read, this story, imagination is far from being dead, my friends, in spite of what has been rumored lately, imagination dead imagine, bah, no difficulty there, and besides it does not take much imagination to invent all that, to fill in future social, political, and scientific gaps

and in any event we know from experience that the future will permit all that to take place, and more, much more that has not yet been anticipated or even been dreamed of by our most eloquent poets, our most daring scientists, our most successful fiction writers, that's for damn sure, yes the unimagined remains to be invented and one need not rely on mathematical predictions, statistical approximations, or complex stochastic theories to shape the future

and personally I don't really care about all that, I am mostly interested in the old guy, or rather I should say we meaning here myself and those who subsequently in this story might get involved with the old man's predicament, I am not alone in this, anything can happen, and others might come into play, but at any rate interested above all in the reasons why he is being sent, banished rather to the colonies, thrown out of our world like a piece of trash, a useless burnt out light bulb, it's the human that concerns me here, but also the coincidental vibrations of life, a question of ethical curiosity on my part, yes a profound and personal need to come to terms with the unexplainable, no not the morbid, why should I, on the contrary, the salubrious, in fact I am almost tempted to say the problematic and the unjust, for it is puzzling, disconcerting indeed to see an old man like him, an extraordinary man in many ways, though quite unpredictable at times, and so unlucky too, being sent to the colonies without any, any

he had a rough life you know, his was a constant struggle for survival and recognition, yes, his life was a series of stumblings, unfortunate stumblings toward his destiny, therefore morally, but also artistically, I feel an obligation, a duty to reveal for posterity the truth of his predicament, to tell, in my own best words, the essentials of his difficult but interesting existence, to relate, as compassionately as I can, with the help of those who knew him well, the story of his misfortunes and déboires

watch that French stuff Federman you say or else I might frustrate my potential readers, that's a chance one must take, after all the old man was born in France, yes like me, coincidentally again, in 1918, as we have already determined, or at least that's as far as one can trace his beginning, born in France, under the regime of Georges Clémenceau in fact, to use a specific point de repère, then Ministre de la Guerre and Président du Conseil, yes under Clémenceau, better known as Le Tigre, if you guys care to verify, Clémenceau who interpreted universal history in terms of the dichotomy between the semites and the aryans, and that's a crucial element in our story, Clémenceau who, you may recall, saved La Belle France from the German invasion and the fiasco of World War I, in 1918, a long time ago, but that's when our old man was born, presumably, on May 15, a Taurus, a real bull with his feet on the ground and his head in the clouds, who had to struggle all his life to conquer vanity and indolence

and of Jewish origin on top of that, not that this fact makes much difference here, not at all, it's quite irrelevant to this story, or barely relevant, but it does raise the interesting scholarly question of whether or not there ever was a Jewish character, a Jewish space-traveler, I mean space-hero

no I'm not going to research the subject, let the likes of Professor Les Cloches and other devotees of futuristic fiction do that kind of scholarly investigation, it's just that it is an interesting question, don't you think, La Question Juive, as Jean-Paul Sartre once put it, however don't start thinking that the old guy is being deported to the colonies for reasons of race or religion, absolutely not, that would be too simplistic, too old-fashioned, too obvious even, good perhaps for olden times but not for our modern age, at least that's what we were told repeatedly by informed sources, and besides by the end of the 20th century, in this story at any rate, all racism has been wiped out, erased from society, nonetheless the real subject of this story remains the expulsion of the old man, our central concern will be to find out why

I am compelled by human compassion, but also by the spirit of creativity, to get to the bottom of this matter, whatever the risks may be, which has been termed, as shall be revealed later, an irrevocable measure

what do you mean you can't wait, don't rush me, yes, yes I know that time is of the essence now as our old man waits at the spaceport in his little antechamber of departure, as he sits resigned on his trunk, that metal box specially designed for space-travel, which contains the last mementos, the vestiges of his life, but remember, in this matter of writing, resolve as one may to keep to the main road some bypaths have an enticement not readily withstood, I am going to err into such bypaths as we progress, it's inevitable, if you guys care to keep me company I shall be glad, at least we can promise ourselves that pleasure which is wickedly said to be in sinning, for a literary sin the divergence will be, how nicely said

and so, even if time is running out, be patient as our old man sits, sits and waits, head between his hands, how else, in a position not unlike that of Rodin's Thinker, except that in his case the legs and arms lack a certain aesthetic harmony suggesting by their clumsy ambivalent positioning that not one but two bodies are sitting here somewhat fused, confused, one into the other like the double exposure on a photograph taken out of focus, therefore apparently redoubled, he sits and waits in the bare antechamber of departure, unknowing, unable, unwilling, but nevertheless an irrevocable measure we were told upon inquiry, and yet nothing, nothing as far as I can tell in the old man's life marked him for the colonies

you say that perhaps I don't know enough about him, about his past, about his private life, his inner self, however impenetrable

it may be, about his psychic makeup, twisted as it may be, his
political inclinations, and even his sexual deviations, if any,
that's possible

you say that the facts, the essential facts of his marginal life may
have escaped me, but one can always guess, invent the facts of a
human existence, I do it all the time for myself, not that he led a
perfect life, an exemplary life, far from it, but he tried, oh how
he tried, that much I was told, yes patience and determination
having been the crutches of his existence, that's well said eh,
and stubbornness the driving force

ah stubbornness, that's what his mother used to deplore the
most about him when he was a child, Quel enfant têtu mon
dieu, une vraie tête de mule, of course in French, his poor
mother, the memory of her face, her sad dark eyes buried in his
subconscious, so that little is known about her, except that
once, on his birthday, when he turned nine, they were very
poor, she bought him un éclair au chocolat, that's about all we
know

not much indeed, his parents were so poor, hardly able to
survive in the years of his youth, and did they suffer, their
entire lives, from hunger and humiliation, before they were
exterminated, and his two sisters too, xxxx out, is how he
always put it

but as the old man explained to us one evening while on the
subject of human suffering, we were having dinner together at
his house, oh many years ago, his lovely wife had fixed a
delicious meal, French cooking naturally, escargots, boeuf à la
crème, mousse au chocolat, the wine was excellent, the conversation lively as always, our friends Moinous and Namredef
were there too that evening, the old man was telling us, as he
had done so many times in the past, about his difficult child-
hood in Paris, about his father who was a starving artist, a
painter, a surrealist painter who suffered from tuberculosis and
was an obsessive gambler on top of that, about his mother, his
poor mother with her sad dark eyes always full of tears, who
took in laundry to help feed the kids, and how the whole family

had to stand in line at the soupe populaire, My mother and father facing toward the wall not to be recognized by the neighbors while my sisters and I were playing games, à cache-cache, hiding behind the other people in line, when suddenly his voice assumed an elegiac tone and he said, One suffers and one suffers from not suffering enough, suffering is never exactly what we feel, my friends, what we call noble or good or true suffering and what moves us is the suffering which we read on the faces of others, or better yet, in portraits, in the face of a statue, in a tragic mask, that suffering has meaning, has being, it is presented as a compact, objective whole which did not await our coming in order to be, and which overflows the consciousness we have of it

that's typical of the kind of statements our old man would make whenever he spoke of his past, always offhandedly, casually, and we were never sure if he was serious or merely teasing us, intellectually I mean, he was so ambivalent, The suffering which I experienced in my life, he continued in the same tone, was never adequate, it always escaped as suffering toward the consciousness of suffering

we didn't argue with him because when he made such statements it was impossible to tell if he was speaking his own thoughts, his own words, or simply abusing the thoughts and words of someone else, our old man was a great borrower of words, a thief of language, he had no scruples in appropriating, misappropriating the words of others, What the hell, he used to say, language is democratic, it belongs to everyone in the same amount and the same basic quality, what one does with it is a matter of personal choice, and personal responsibility

this belief may indeed have been his primary sin, but also his most stubborn conviction, and now, now, if the night passes quietly tomorrow he will be on his way to the colonies, that's how it begins, as to what will happen next, I don't know yet, nor does anyone else

II

The colonies, as will be eventually explained, were set up around 1994, or that's the date I was given, no I don't think it too obvious, or too soon, there is nothing symbolic, nothing premature in that date, don't start making all sorts of literary connections, it's simply that I have to work within a logical time span from the present so that my old guy can be born in 1918, like my father, or even like me, question of synchronicity

all progeny real or fictitious, are verbal extensions in time and in space, and that my dead father and the old man should have the same date of birth as myself, or that my father and myself should have the same birthdate as the old man, is purely coincidental within the creative license of this story, and may have no bearing whatsoever on the unfolding of the narrative, after all history, as a friend once wrote, is a dream already dreamt and destroyed

but that coincidence, that doubleness of the old man, becomes acceptable and even explainable, historically and genetically, when one realizes that my young dead father, he was 42 when they exterminated him, in those days it was not uncommon, did not have time to become a father to his son, me in other words, and that today he, my father, could be the son of his

son, question of temporal readjusting and familial overlapping,
or is it the reverse

you may wonder why the need to go into my own background,
my own sordid life, to tell the story of the old guy, all fiction is
based, to some extent, on the author's own experiences,
whether lived or imagined, transposed into the life of his characters, it always works this way, not blood relations, ink relations

just reread Proust or Céline or the great Gabriel Garcia Mar-
quez for familial overlapping, then you'll see what I mean, the
undoubling or redoubling of personalities, it's all there in the
opening pages when it says, Then it would begin to seem
unintelligible, as the thoughts of a former existence must be to a
reincarnate spirit, the subject of my book would separate itself
from me, leaving me free to choose whether I would form part
of it or not

or, Here we are, alone again, it's all so slow, so heavy, so sad,
I'll be old soon, then at last it will be over

or better yet, Many years later, as he faced the firing squad,
Colonel Aureliano Buendia was to remember that distant afternoon when his father took him to discover ice

yes that's how it always begins, and in the case of our old man,
Many years would pass before he would reach his destination,
perhaps many more than had already passed since he left the
place which was to become his destination, for unknowingly,
the day he stepped out of the closet of his survival and took the
first step of his journey, away from where life was given to him,
he had also taken the first step of his return to the place where
life would be taken away from him, therefore 1918, it has to be
the date of his birth, even if chronologically it seems implausible, otherwise if I throw the story further into the past then
dates and events will not coincide properly, and if, quite arbi-
trarily, I propel the story further into the future, say for the
sake of futuristic credibility in the year 2033 or 2044, or even

beyond, in the cosmicomic future of the space age as it will be known some day, then my old man will be too old, too old that is in terms of the present, our present, but also in terms of the logic of his fictional existence for him to have experienced some of the events, tragic historical events especially, and comitragic too, I would like him to have experienced during his lifetime on earth

for instance the laughable Treaty of Versailles, the pitiful fiasco of the League of Nations, the failed Chinese revolution of 1927 and the long march of Mao Tse-Tung, slim Lindbergh across the Atlantic solo, the Crash and the Great Depression and the mass suicides of the ruined capitalists, the burning of the Reichstag, the sad debacle of the Spanish Civil War and Picasso's gray Guernica in 1937, World War II, the Maginot Line, the Battle of the Bulge where Carl Lester Bumpus was killed, the Vichy Government, the bombing of Pearl Harbor on December 7, Pierre Laval's political machinations, Nazi persecutions of the Jews and the concentration camps

that's an important item which must never be forgotten, yes my old man was there, he experienced the Holocaust, that beautifully sad affair for art as it was once called, in a way he was a survivor, an escapee, way back then, he endured that humiliating experience and somehow managed to survive it, by extension one might say, and that's crucial, central to our story, I think

for the stupefying truth is that the Holocaust is the epic event of the 20th century never striking bottom in the resonance of its tragic fact, no question about that, even the most banal aspects of life in the camps, the most basic, the most innocent questions one asks about the daily routine of the deportees, such as did they brush their teeth, did they cut their nails, did they blow their noses in the camps, did they make love, did they ever smile, reach the level of Greek tragedy, or at least the level of the Theater of the Absurd, and therefore should not be left unanswered, especially now

this way to the showers, Ladies and Gentlemen and Dear

Children, remember Borowski, for it is the law of the camps that people going to their death must be deceived to the very end, it's an old historical trick, Here little boys little girls have a piece of chocolate to take away your fear, it only takes three minutes for the gas to choke you, deception is the only permissible form of charity in the process of extermination, Dostoevsky, you may recall, learned that lesson on the morning of December 22, 1849, when he faced the firing squad, true, he survived, but did he learn, oh did he learn, and millions and millions of others too learned that painful lesson since that day, and who knows, the space colonies may also be another form of charitable deception

but if we deal with this matter of the camps at all, it will have to be clear that the central concern is not the extermination of the deportees, including the old guy's entire family, incidentally, father, mother, and sisters too, but the erasure of that extermination as a central event, and it is, I believe, the old man's ambivalence toward this erasure that charges his life emotionally and informs its risks, but perhaps I am anticipating too much

nonetheless these are some of the events I have in mind, but many others too that need be remembered, for instance the first atomic blast, D-Day, the cold war and bebop, the public burning of the Rosenbergs, the Iron Curtain, Existentialism and Structuralism

oh you people don't think I should go into that old stuff again, well only marginally, we'll deal with that psychophilocrap peripherally, after all it left its mark

the hippie movement of the '60s, the old man was even thrown in jail during the student unrest, he was younger then of course, and passionate, no not in Berkeley, not at the Sorbonne in May '68, but in Buffalo, yes Buffalo, and not because he was a radical fanatic or a political guru, certainly not, it was just a fluke, Moinous, Namredef, and I rushed to the Queen City to bail him out when we heard about the arrest he was visiting an old friend in Buffalo, the armpit of America as he referred to it later, the campus of the university, known then as the Yellow Submarine, was occupied by the police, 400 toughs who carried their revolvers low-slung and chewed gum from the side of their mouths, riot police called in to preserve Law & Order because the kids were throwing rocks and Coca-Cola bottles at the windows of the buildings and painting obscenities in red on the walls to express their disagreement with certain policies of the government, long forgotten now, Nixon sucks, Agnew beats his wife, the C.I.A. eats shit, Make Love Not War, les structures ne descendent pas dans la rue, this one from a French major, Godot Go Home, Burn Baby Burn, and other such relevant slogans

the old man and his friend, a poet-professor, an eccentric by the name of Marrant, who never gained the recognition he deserved and who jumped off the Peace Bridge in 1998, no not out of despair but because of an excess of creativity, therefore needless to go into the details of his life and work, though one should perhaps mention the title of his important and controversial study of what he called Laughterature, the old man and his friend, I was saying, were walking past the university campus in the early evening, gesticulating like two disrupted puppets in the middle of an argument, about poetry, I suppose, or philosophy, when they decided to take a look at the commotion

just to see what's going on, for the fun of it, what the hell, as the cops and the kids were confronting each other in front of the library, throwing rocks at each other, or whatever they could get their hands on in this troubled academic environment, chairs, desks, typewriters, books, hardbound especially from the rare books collection, bookcases, bicycles, half-chewed hamburgers and hot dogs, excrement even, and there he was, there they were the two of them, curious middle-aged gentlemen already graying at the temples, towering above the mob, they were both very tall, shouting slogans at the cops with the kids, denouncing the government, accusing those who fix bayonet, those who statue liberty, those who can you hear,

those who float and never sink, those who hamletize and vietna-
mize, those who think they think, those who masturbate with
gloves on, letting their poetic imagination run wild, exposing
those who love it or leave it, those who have feathers, those who
bumpersticker, those who have their daily meals six times a day
while others, the poor slobs, have their daily bread approx-
imately once a week, and they shouted against those who, those
who, those who screw in the dark with their eyes closed,
improvising as they went along, full of good spirit, having a
ball, glad to be here, thrilled to be part of this great youthful
mass

fantastic, what a scene, hey it's not often one has a chance to get
involved like this, and the old guy grabbed another bicycle
which had just flown past his head and threw it back at the cops
hitting one of them squarely on the bridge of the nose with the
handlebar and the poor cop screamed as blood spurted out on
his fellowcops, and before the old man knew what was happening he was clubbed on the head, contusively, and dragged into a
K9 wagon, dragged by the feet on the ground and thrown into
the wagon like a sack of potatoes while he cursed the cops

our old guy was a rather free-speaking fellow, bilingually of
course, Hey you motherfuckers, enculés, bastards, you bunch
of brutes, enfoirés, sales cons, get your hands off me, protest-
ing, explaining that he was not really involved, just passing by,
you idiots, couillons, pisspots, don't you see I'm in the wrong
place at the wrong time, not unlike him by the way, just a
coincidence

meanwhile his poet-friend got lost in the shuffle and escaped
arrest, but the old man, wearing an expensive leather coat lined
with fur, a gift from his wife for his birthday that very year, it
was a cold March day incidentally, was led to jail along with 44
young radical students, the Buffalo 45 they were called, led
handcuffed by two giant cops who held him by the arms, one of
whom, somewhat less of a brute than the others, in fact could
have easily passed for your typical friendly neighbor under
different circumstances, nervous and twitchy even with his

revolver low-slung, felt sorry for this rather distinguished-looking middle-aged gentleman who seemed obviously out of place in this tumult

It's gonna be all right Sir, don't you worry about a thing, Sir, it's just that we have to do our duty

and our old man, casually, Oh I'm not worried, I've seen worse in my life, much worse

Oh, puzzled the cop

Yep four years in a concentration camp during the last war, and I survived as you can see, you must understand my friend, the old man added with a disarming smile on his face, that one must never blame medicine for having failed to cure mortality

totally thrown off guard the friendly policeman was taken aback, he felt so embarrassed, so shitty, when he heard that, he instinctively loosened his grip on the old man's arm thus suggesting, I presume, that he should perhaps try to escape while there was still time

By the way, the nervous cop asked imploringly, are you a citizen, and this time with a truly concerned tone of voice, having noticed, and how could he miss it, the heavy unmistakable French accent which the old man had never managed to lose, even twenty or thirty years after he came to America, his friends often accused him teasingly of deliberately cultivating his French accent for sentimental and practical reasons, Because, the concerned cop hesitated, you know sometimes they deport foreigners who, who, well you know what I mean Sir

Of course I am a citizen, replied our old man sounding prouder of this fact than he intended, and so off to jail he went with the 44 young radicals who were sporting arrogant long greasy hair, bushy beards, and dirty nails, and the next morning all the newspapers in the country, the New York Times, the Chicago Tribune, the Boston Globe, the Washington Post, all the biggies, but also the Miami Herald, the Elkhart Truth, the Peoria

Post, the Kirksville Gazette, in other words all the hicktown dailies, including of course the local Buffalo Evening News and Courier-Express, and later that week even Newsweek and Time Magazine, carried the story and the old man's picture behind bars with the following caption, Unidentified middle-aged agent provocateur leads hippie mob against police, forty-five arrested and charged with trespassing, rioting, use of obscene language and gestures, civil disobedience, resisting arrest, and conduct unbecoming in public

somehow the old man found himself appointed leader of the Buffalo 45, because of his age, I assume, and his obvious maturity, he had a huge grin on his face in the picture in Newsweek, not unlike him to smile in a situation such as this one, he was known for his scorn of authority and his sense of humor

his wife's mother, a nice but conservative widow who lived in California at the time, Los Angeles, telephoned her daughter immediately when she saw, by chance, the picture of her son-in-law behind bars in her copy of Newsweek, I told you, I always told you he was a communist, the old lady shouted into the telephone, she was quite perturbed, I warned you the day you were married, you should have listened to me, what are you going to do now, you must think of yourself, your future, after all you're still a young woman

But mother, Mother dear, you don't understand

to no avail, the old lady had never been too fond nor too appreciative of her son-in-law, on the contrary, rather suspicious of his idiosyncratic behavior and what she called his distant show of emotions towards others, not aware that he acted this way only with her, as a kind of protective measure, With old folks, he used to say, one must always keep one's distances, they have a way of stifling you

from the moment they first met things didn't click too well between them, he locked her out of his private self, as mother-in-law she was, to say the least, predictably standard in her attitude, inquisitive and stubborn, humorless and advisory, and always so proper, so ladylike, when the day came for him to meet his future mother-in-law, It's unavoidable darling, his wife-to-be explained, he insisted that the meeting take place on neutral ground, I don't care where, in a bar, on a bus, in a Turkish bath, but not, I insist, absolutely not, as it was originally proposed, at the old lady's house, and so they had lunch together, the two of them, in a stuffy Beverly Hills restaurant, there were awkward moments of silence during which the old lady scrutinized him through her bifocal glasses with a slight trembling of the head, he was wearing for the occasion a striped necktie and his one and only tweed jacket which was worn through at the elbows, during the entire lunch he managed to keep his elbows below the table, not a very comfortable way to enjoy what turned out to be a halfway decent meal of broccoli soup, chicken à la king, cucumber salad, and rice pudding, for some reason he never forgot the menu on this particular day, but since the old lady insisted on picking up the tab, the inconvenience and uneasiness of this first encounter became almost tolerable

in any event, they held him a week in jail, a sobering week of tasteless baloney sandwiches and insipid coffee without cream or sugar, released finally on $2,000 bail, the money raised by an emergency activist group organized by his faithful friends Moinous and Namredef, quite remarkable since more than $90,000 was needed to free the 45 prisoners, and that without the legal expenses, in those days political solidarity was at its peak

the day the Buffalo 45 were released a huge demonstration was organized and June Fanon, yes the famous movie star, who was then a notorious political activist, as so many movie stars were in those days, flew in from Hollywood to make a passionate speech about human rights and civil liberties, what a woman, she stood on a platform hastily constructed for the occasion on Lafayette Square

of course the old guy was there, he wouldn't have missed for anything in the world this chance to see June Fanon in person she stood on the platform in a mini-skirt and leather boots, the style that year, her reddish hair flowing wildly in the breeze, legs spread apart in sensual defiance, and shouted as an opener to the thousands assembled on the square, Hello There Fellow Bums, she was gorgeous, and so self-assured, the crowd of aroused students, concerned professors, and troubled citizens reacted with spontaneous enthusiasm

the old guy stood in the front row, center, looking up at June, having a splendid view of her intense liberal position, but when he was recognized as the leader of the Buffalo 45, the organizers immediately asked him to come up on the platform, the crowd applauded and chanted, Hello There Fellow Bum, as he walked center stage and sat directly behind June, quite excited about that, he was still wearing his now popularly recognizable fur-lined leather coat, from his seat he waved at the crowd, June walked over to the old man, applauding with the crowd, and put her arms around him, it was a beautiful moment

then she went back to the microphone, legs provocatively spread apart, and again shouted, Hello There Fellow Bums, the crowd went wild, wild with youthful arrogance in its stand against the government, against police brutality, against the oil companies, and I.B.M., and Xerox, and Dow Chemical, and General Motors, against police action in the Far East, against free enterprise, Wall Street, R.O.T.C., and all the other oppressive institutions of the time

tears welled up in the old man's eyes, sentimental tears of solidarity, Hello There Fellow Bums, June Fanon repeated like a chant with her All-American voice, and this time the crowd exploded into uncontrollable hysteria, she was unable to add another word as the cops, lined twelve deep on the periphery of the square, charged into the crowd, and quickly the old man's tears turned to lachrymatory pains when the tear gas bombs hit the mob, hundreds were wounded as the police, reinforced by national guards and state troopers, broke up the demonstration clubbing left and right indiscriminately, but this time our old guy managed to escape without a scratch, and without being noticed, with June Fanon, holding hands as they ran away from this ugly scene, never to set foot again in Buffalo, they both swore

but let me assure you, Namredef and Moinous checked on this, the old man is not being deported to the colonies because of this ancient political involvement, he was totally cleared eventually, but nonetheless that's the kind of historical event he experienced

and many others too, for instance the assassination of John F. Kennedy in 1963, which he watched on television with millions of other stunned Americans, and of Bobby Kennedy a few years later, in 1968, wasn't it, also shown on television live, and the rise and fall of Richard Nixon, and the historic visit of the Egyptian President to Jerusalem, in 1977, what a day that was when Anwar Sadat and Menachem Begin embraced in front of the wailing wall, and the fabulous evening in 1978 when the great Muhammad Ali regained his heavyweight title for the third time by defeating Leon Spinks in fifteen tough rounds, that too was an historical moment, our old man was there that night, and the total eclipse of the sun on that Monday, February 26, 1979, our old man may never again see one in his lifetime, at least not from this planet, though, who knows, perhaps from the colonies he might see a total eclipse of the earth, if that's any consolation

and there is more that our old man experienced, the disastrous Italian revolution and the burning of the Vatican in 1989, no the Pope did not survive, poor fellow, he burnt alive on the roof of St. Peter at dawn while blessing humanity, I was not there in person but some witnesses, friends of the old man, told me about it, but that's not all, the first 18 hole championship golf course on the moon designed by Jack Nicklaus under government contract and where the First Universe Open was played in 1991

oh you people didn't know Jack Nicklaus designed golf courses in space, yes of course after he was forced to retire from competition because of a bad knee which caused a permanent loss of his superb swing, by then he had earned over 60 million dollars, and was still going strong when he twisted his leg in a sand trap at Pebble Beach

you should have seen the shots these golfers hit on the moon, 1700 to 1800 yard drives, in the remote valleys of the Sea of Tranquillity, what, that's all you say, 1700 or 1800 yard drives on the moon, what do you mean that's all, have you ever tried to hit even 200 or 230 yards, and I don't mean on the moon, but here on earth, you guys are kidding yourselves if you think golf is an old man's game

our old geezer could teach you something about that, yes indeed, he was a golf fanatic all his life, and damn good at it, played to a three handicap in his days, though he never managed to break par, that was his one great disappointment, he always used to say, Before I die I must shoot one round under par, but now I doubt he will ever make it

it's true, however, that these space golfers are using special extrasuper gravitational moonballs, Molitors XL Plus 3000

and that's not all, no that's not all our old man experienced before he received his notice of deportation, the first baby born in space, a joint Russian-American venture which produced a beautiful girl appropriately named Katerina Ivanovna Elisabeth Venus, and the first artificial strawberries and bananas, I mention these because he loves strawberries and bananas my old man, ah yes the orgies of bananas and strawberries in his life, but I doubt he will ever again delight in such delicacies, natural or artificial, once he reaches the colonies

and so much more, yes so much more that concerns us all, but especially my old man

such as the tragic but not unexpected earthquake of 1990 in Southern California which wiped out most of Los Angeles, only Orange County and Pasadena were left intact for some strange mystical reason, some people even claimed it was politically engineered, yes most of Los Angeles and all the sunny little communities in a ninety mile radius, totally demolished, as far north as lovely Santa Barbara where, it should be mentioned, our old guy spent many happy years once upon a time playing tennis, golf, writing poetry, and living a life of leisure

he even fell in love there in the late 1950s, madly in love, with the woman he eventually married, his one and only wife, as far as is known, a splendid woman of rare sensibility and patient understanding who brought out in him extreme states of uxoriousness, blue eyes, black hair, a great beauty, and a fine and generous person indeed who paid off all his gambling debts the day after they were married, a gesture which touched him very much, a marvelous woman who will undoubtedly play an important role in this story if we can get in touch with her, and to whom he remained married for some thirty years, damn right that's constancy for you, until the Dismarital Law of 1990 was passed, same year as the California earthquake, and all legal marriages were dissolved as a birth control measure

he was reading a poem to her in their summer cottage, in Cassis, when the news about the Dismarital Law was announced on televista, yes the old man is a poet, and a novelist too, like me, and of some reputation, that will certainly have to be discussed eventually, and yes they had a little country retreat, nothing fancy, just a simple rustic folly, as they called it

he was reading a love poem to her which he had just finished, somewhat erotic, which recalled in metaphoric terms how the two of them first indulged, years ago, in the sexual act, with all the furor and passion they felt for one another, no it was not the first time for either of them, of course not, they had had lots of previous sexual experiences, but it was the first time together, they met one afternoon in an elevator and instantly reacted to the electricity of their mutual desire, that's a metaphor he used in the poem, Short Circuit was the title, later that evening she came to his place, a crummy one room apartment near the university where he was writer in residence, he was poor then, barely earning enough to survive, but as he was fond of saying about the condition of his bohemian life, La vie de l'artiste c'est de la merde, always reverting to his native tongue whenever he felt philosophical, and they made love, she gave herself without

resistance, without the least hesitation, and without even ex-
changing a single word with him during the act, a silent recip-
rocal understanding one might say, deeply felt, she was not the
garrulous type, but what a woman, he loved her very much

Do you remember, he asked pausing in the middle of reading
his new poem, Yes I do, she reached for his hand, We must
have connected at least six or seven times that night, together,
he reminded her while trying to replay in his mind the intimate
scene, or at least its ultimate climax, And that's the meaning of
the final image in my poem, The window burst into dust and
beyond infinity the sun collided six times with the night, he
explained, but his explanation was not necessary, she had
understood and was obviously moved, and ready to show her
affection when, suddenly, the newscaster announced that the
Dismarital Law had been approved unanimously by the members of The World Congress for the Protection of Humanity,
WCPH, as it is known in this story, and that consequently all
legal marriages were dissolved immediately and all married
couples were to separate, regardless of age, social status,
physical condition, length of association, or emotional involvement

this was the first step toward what is now called triangular
sexual accommodation, or if you prefer triple organic relationship, three males or three females, or else two and one of
each sex, though lately in some parts of the world these sexual
accommodations have been expanding beyond the triple set, up
to group-five, and even group-seven or nine, yes always an odd
number for obvious practical reasons of sentimental harmony

these then are some of the events I would like my old guy to
have witnessed and experienced here on earth, in this story, but
many others too, especially the death of such famous people as
Marcel Proust, Paul Valéry, Aristide Briand, Pirandello,
Kafka, Leon Trotsky, Fernandel, Hitler, and Marshal Pétain,
well famous or infamous, Gertrude Stein, Boris Vian, Charlie
Parker, Céline, Marcel Duchamp, Charles de Gaulle, Edith
Piaf, Lumumba, Picasso, Franco, Jean-Paul Sartre, Vladimir
Nabokov, Campbell Tatham

Campbell who, you ask, Tatham, oh you people have never heard of him, a close friend of the old guy who departed prematurely and who for a time had a strong intellectual influence on his work, but also the death of Fidel Castro, Johnny Carson, and O.J., and Professor Marrant with whom our old man shared many hilarious thoughts, and Joe Murez, Sylvia Plath, and Hombre della Pluma, and Monoeil, to name only a few who come to mind at this time and who had a marked direct or indirect impact on the old man's life, therefore it is understandable why I have to give 1994 as the date for the birth of the space colonies, otherwise

what do you mean it's not plausible, historically and scientifically speaking, not possible, on the contrary, what do you think this is a pseudorealistic story that pretends to record facts, how narrow-minded and backward you people are, how enslaved to your realism, Edgar Allan Poe was so right in his time when he called nascent 19th century realism that pitiable stuff invented by merchants for the depiction of decayed cheeses, what do you think modern writers are, milkmen or something, that's what my old man would certainly answer if you were to raise that question of credibility with him, no it is not that implausible, that preposterous, nor that far-fetched, our ultra-modern technology is quite capable of such extraordinary ventures into space, and besides the establishment of these colonies, as predicted by such clairvoyant writers of the past as Cyrano de Bergerac, Jules Verne, H.G. Wells, Charles Lutwidge Dodgson, H.P. Lovecraft, or of the future, such as my young friend Joe Francavilla, is not only possible by 1994, not only desirable and advisable, but essential in terms of our lousy present-day morality, not to mention the many social and cultural advantages such far-out establishments would bring to the world

after all isn't it the role of fiction, and I don't mean science-fiction only, to alter reality for the better, the writer may not be as privileged as the scientist nowadays, or perhaps he is, who knows, for this oblique witness of reality must at the same time seek and avoid precision, he knows that the reality of imagination is more real than reality without imagination, and besides reality as such has never really interested anyone, it is and has always been a form of disenchantment, our old man would say, quite rightly, were he to be asked, for he often pondered that question during his life, what makes reality fascinating at times is the imaginary catastrophe which hides behind it, the writer knows this and exploits it whereas the scientist tends to ignore it willfully, and this is why the writer must seek and avoid precision simultaneously, which may cause him to suffer violent strokes of delirium and typographiphobia, but what the hell, scientific precision, on the other hand, is always antidelirious and calmative, thus from a purely evocative point of view the creation of the space colonies is not as implausible as you people may think if you consider, for a moment, that by the end of the 1950s one could fly from Paris to New York, let's say, in less than eight hours

big deal you say, okay big deal, but by the middle of the 1970s, a mere 15 years or so later, what's 15 years in the long painful history of mankind, one could make the same journey by suprasuprasonic jets and arrive in New York even before one had left Paris, permitting the fortunate traveler to have lunch in a swanky three star restaurant with a fine bottle of Château Margaux or Château Latour 1959 before departing, and breakfast, bagel lox and cream cheese for instance, upon arriving, thus reversing the natural order of human meals and upsetting the delicate balance of gastronomical taste, how does that strike you

leaves you cold, all right, but are you aware that by the end of the 1970s or thereabouts, cosmonauts and astronauts were already rendezvousing in space while other daring space pioneers were shooting golf balls on the moon or playing volleyball in the ionosphere, no I am not exaggerating, just consult the newspapers of the time, and are you aware that only a few short years later the exploration and conquest of Mars and Venus and other planets in our solar system by such adventurous corporations as Coca Cola Unlimited and I. T. T. Transuniversal had reached, in spatial terms that is, the first stages of agricultural exploitation and robot domestication, soon after, in fact, the first direct telephone conversation between the moon and earth took place, don't you remember when the first American astronaut, how quickly we forget his name, set foot on the moon and called the White House in Washington with special hookups to the oval office to speak with the President of the United States of America, it was Johnson, I think, or was it Nixon already, that sonofabitch, Nixon yes of course, I stand corrected, what a day that was

the event was televised in color and live all over the world, though a lot of incredulous people thought it was a hoax, a television put-on, a phony Hollywoodian production à la Orson Welles, Mister President Sir, the astronaut said in a grave ponderous voice, I am on the moon, the entire world held its breath, How does it look up there Man, asked the President diplomatically moved, and that day our old man reflected gloomily, as I did myself and billions of others must have too, on how millenniums and millenniums of human dreams went down the drain with that historic phone call and that giant step for humanity

dreams that go as far back in time as the unfathomable moment when the first primate cracked his ribcage during the Lower Pleistocene era to rise from a four-legged position to a biped posture and screaming with pain into the prehistoric wilderness launched humanity on its long march toward civilization and beyond

toward the invention of the wheel, the bronze age, the Hanging Gardens of Babylon, the Egyptian Pyramids, Greek mythology and the Oedipus complex, the burning of Rome, the first chamber pot, Christianity, yes all that down the drain

the invention of the sonnet, the Great Wall of China, Gutenberg's printing press, the discovery of America, down the drain

the Inquisition, the Reformation, the Restoration, Pascal's calculating machine, Descartes' cogito ergo sum, down the drain

le fil à couper le beurre, Newton's apple, la sauce hollandaise, Goethe's Faust, the Napoleonic wars, the French revolution, the industrial revolution, the rise of bourgeois society, the Guillotine, Karl Marx's assault on Capitalism, down the drain

Les Fleurs du mal, Darwin's theory of evolution, Crime and Punishment, the laws of thermodynamics, realism, naturalism, positivism, determinism, the Death of God, the Eiffel Tower, down the drain with that historic phone call from the moon

the quantum theory, $E = mc^2$, Kittyhawk, constructivism, Dadaism, Sein und Zeit, slim Lindbergh across the Atlantic in the Spirit of St. Louis, Mein Kampf, Madagascar for the Jews, Hiroshima or Harry S Truman's the Buck Stops Here, D-Day, the Holocaust and German gas chambers, down the drain with that giant step for humanity up there on the moon

the silent generation, la littérature engagée, le nouveau roman, Tel Quel, our old man's journey to America across the Atlantic on the S.S. Marine Jumper to confront the American-way-of-life, Waiting for Godot, the Beatles, Women's Lib and the Pill, the Bay of Pigs, The Death of the Novel and Other Stories, Double or Nothing, Null Set and Other Stories, Point Omega, the Concord, Beaubourg, Gravity's Rainbow, Nuclear Love, clonery and corpomancy, the conquest of space, Star Wars, Apocalypse Now, etcetera, etcetera, all that down the drain

how justified he was our old man to feel gloomy that day, when the moon spoke to the Earth, for indeed we were but a small step, yes a small step and not a giant step from that telephone call to the establishment of the space colonies, in 1994, as they are proposed and presented in this story, for as my old friend Sam once said, It's the end that is the worst, no, it's the beginning that is the worst, then the middle, then the end, in the end it's the end that is the worst, so why argue the point, why resist the inevitable, especially at a time when it is so urgent to get to the bottom of this matter and find out, once and for all, if our old man can be saved, or at least if his imminent departure can be postponed until all the facts are known about his deportation

III

Time is running out as the old man sits resigned in the narrow antechamber of departure, final closet of my earthly life, he calls it, head between his hands, the buzzing of his past in his ears, with his faithful dog, Sam, a droopy thoroughbred Dalmatian, crouched like a sphinx at his feet, the only living company allowed him until the final moment

oh no, my Dear Madam, the dog will not be permitted to go with him, dogs are not deported to the space colonies, not yet, they are still considered inferior creatures, of little use in space, I suppose the poor animal will be exterminated once the spaceship leaves the launching pad, at midnight, as is customary every year on new year's eve since 1994

for in spite of the many changes that have taken place in our world, certainly for the better of the human condition, our attitude toward animals remains ambiguous, oppressive rather, and even though many domestic animals have adjusted to a higher standard of life with man and participate quite willingly in the new moral and social code of behavior, and even in the new sexual accommodation system, which is not the case however with wild animals many of whom still refuse to be domesticated and therefore remain unsocialized and uncivilized, the question of animal rights and animal welfare is the cause of many debates nowadays

and our old man himself, who his entire life was fiercely involved in liberal causes, argued, not long ago, when called upon to testify as an expert witness in a controversial case of animal rape by a human, that of a female French poodle who cohabited with a nice elderly lady and who was brutally assaulted and despicably used in the staircase of the apartment building where the two of them lived, that the higher the order of animal life, the greater its right to define its own state of existence and protect its own body

Our whole moral and legal tradition, the old guy declared emphatically to the members of the jury, in Baltimore where the case was being heard, is founded on the assumption that there is an unbridgeable gap between humans and animals giving us the right to own and exploit them, and as he spoke these words the old man stared at the accused, a depraved-looking man who was gnawing nervously at his fingernails like a squirrel on a chestnut, Yes Ladies and Gentlemen of the jury, he shouted, and even abuse them without reference to their best interests, however, he continued, facing the audience this time, if our scientists, our social workers, and especially our animal therapists now tell us that animals are different from us only in degree, his voice rose with emotion, and if the exemplary relationship I entertain with my own dog, Sam, can be respectfully presented here as an objective illustration, and he pointed in the direction of Sam who was sprawled in a corner of the courtroom near the judge's bench, chewing quietly on the court reporter's shoe, but who raised one droopy eye and wagged his tail when he heard his name, Yes if Sam can be cited as an exceptional case in point, then our exploitation of animals carries far more serious implications than we have been willing to admit, for we are confronting in this instance a threat to cosmic unity that embraces not only minerals, plants, and animals, but humans as well, the whole of Nature as a cooperative enterprise is in question here, Ladies and Gentlemen the large crowd of partisan spectators, including representatives of the mass media, who were occupying every available seat in the federal courtroom, many of whom had brought with them their favorite pets, dogs, cats, monkeys, birds, insects, and even one rather large but friendly alligator on a leash, began to stir approvingly while the attorney for the defense of the rapist, bearlike in his movements and obviously bigoted, threw his papers on the floor in disgust, upon which Sam promptly took a leak in full sight of everyone

Have you ever heard anything more outrageous, seen anything more disgusting, the angry attorney mumbled to his assistant, a lanky red-haired fellow restless like a dehydrated ostrich but who seemed moved by the old man's forceful argument, What the hell is happening to our world, sneered the attorney as he hurled his briefcase at Sam

the old man ignored him, and so did Sam who was back in his corner licking his penis

One more such demonstration, the judge said pointing his finger at the attorney, and I shall hold you in contempt of court, Go on Sir, the judge added turning to the old man

Your Honor, the old man continued slowly and deliberately now addressing the bench, what the new scientific and psychological discoveries about animals demand is not more justification for protecting them, but the recognition that animals, domesticated or not, have a right to a decent life regardless of their usefulness to humanity, he paused and cleared his throat, have a right to walk our streets in safety and enjoy their animal freedom without having to fear for their bodies

the spectators burst into applause, the judge stood up and banged his gavel again and again while shouting, Order in the court, order in the court, even the pets were barking and meowing and squeaking and growling joyfully, the judge finally managed to restore order when he threatened to clear the room the old man then concluded, still speaking directly to the judge who, back in his chair, was straightening his gown, For if we recognize in our legal system that individual lives have value, and we may not vivisect one Mongoloid to save ten normal humans, why then, I ask, even though we feel emotionally that animals' lives have value to them, why then have we not granted those lives any real protection, and he turned toward the French poodle who was sitting innocently at the feet of the prosecutor, any real protection, the old man reiterated, in our anthropocentric judicial system

Bravo, Bravo, a damn good argument, someone shouted in the crowd, and this time he received a standing ovation, in spite of the judge's repeated warnings that he would not tolerate such disorderly displays of parti pris, the old man waved at the audience as he stepped down from the witness stand and walked out of the courtroom followed by faithful Sam who was obviously pleased with his master's performance, and who wagged his superb tail and exposed his unusual canine perfection as if parading in an elegant dog show while he glanced sideways at the French poodle, and no doubt the old man spoke with conviction and the firm belief that in his own relationship with his dog he had granted Sam from the beginning full equality, full human privileges and liberties in their coexistence

however, as he left the courtroom, the old man admitted to Moinous and Namredef who were accompanying him that day that quite frankly he had found the whole scene rather idiotic, for deep inside he really didn't give a damn about man's inhumanity to animals, What do I care about animalistic welfare, he said shrugging his shoulders, I have enough difficulties taking care of my own survival, what interested him in this particular case, and the reason therefore why he had agreed to testify, was the metaphoric system it implied, and also the chance it offered him to demonstrate publicly the perfection of his personal relationship with Sam

how fond he was of his dog, You spoil that dumb animal, his wife would say, before they were legally separated, in 1990, as a result of the Dismarital Law, and indeed for 51 years, that's how old Sam is now, no not that unbelievable since recent medical research in the field of animal longevity has produced remarkable results, unfortunately not as successful yet in the case of human life, and for good reasons, since many concerned middle-aged people have been arguing, What if in the near future life-extension becomes commonplace, what will we do with all these great-great-grandparents, will they hold on to their jobs forever, and if they don't, who will support them, and what if the first technology to prevent aging is incredibly expensive, will that mean that only the wealthy will be able to turn back the clock of life, or that the government will select the future Methuselahs based on its own criteria, such as intelligence, race, talent, or perhaps even political affiliation, that is an untenable solution, therefore it is understandable why research in human longevity has been bogged down, but not so for animals, because in most cases humans really don't care if their pets outlive them, and so for 51 years now the old man and his dog have had a most intimate, a most delightful relationship

not that of master and servile companion, but rather that of platonic lovers, Sam always slept at the foot of his bed, on his own pillow, cuddled in a baby blanket, always traveled with him as a full fare passenger on trains, boats, buses, airplanes, participated in all his sporting activities, and during the meals he sat patiently next to the old man drooling profusely as he waited for that piece of meat, and especially those French fried potatoes they both loved so much, to be thrown to him, stealthily behind the wife's back, and which the alert animal would catch in full flight as gracefully as Willie Mays caught fly balls when he played centerfield for the Giants, remember

Sam had been so overprotected for half a century that he had never had occasion for sexual intercourse, not even with a member of his own species, therefore a 51-year-old Dalmatian languidly crouched now at the feet of his human friend in that dismal antechamber of departure frowning his instinctual animal anguish in the face of a great mystery that escapes his comprehension that's how the situation stands at this point, or at least that's what the narrators of this story have reported to me after they last saw the old man and his dog in the antechamber of departure, Namredef and Moinous who shall soon play a more prominent role as the plot unfolds, for it is from them, Namredef and Moinous, inseparable narrators of my story, but also devoted lifelong friends and acolytes of the old guy, who have been investigating the situation, that all information is received

perhaps I should have clarified this sooner, though it has been implicit all along, that my role here is merely that of a scribe, that of a detached reporter, and that in fact I am only an intermediary figure in the telling of this story, a secondhand teller if you wish, as I have been on several occasions in the past, that this is so will become evident, as we proceed, self-explanatory even, since I have lost touch, in a manner of speaking, with the old man for many years now

yes, as a matter of fact, since that day in Buffalo when he ran off with June Fanon, holding hands you may recall, after that pathetic political rally, we were there that day, in person, Namredef, Moinous, and I, and it was then we realized that political understanding is but a series of second thoughts

What, oh the French poodle, yes she won her case, the rapist was deported to the colonies, but by then the old guy was no longer involved nor concerned with this case, il avait d'autres chiens à fouetter, as Moinous explained, and besides it was just a minor digression in the course of things, don't look for hidden meanings in what I report, this is not a do-it-yourself Tantalus-kit

as for our old friend and June Fanon, I learned later that they had a passionate love affair, a scandalous love affair, even though they kept it very secret, the old man was still married at the time, and his wife found out about it, not indirectly, but from the old man himself, yes he told her, confessed the whole thing, perhaps out of guilt, or out of sincerity, what a mess that was it lasted only a few weeks, the love affair, four or five at most, but what intensity, yes what madness, De la folie pure, is the way Namredef and Moinous put it to me, oui in French since we were sitting in a café in Montparnasse when they reported the matter, La Closerie des Lilas, I remember, where the old man told us he had had some fabulous meals with Sam Beckett, over the years, their favorite meeting place, they were buddies, Sam and the old guy, first name basis, but of course, as he explained to me once, Beckett, ah he's an exceptional being, a kind of archangel, he comes from above, me, I come from below, from the cave, they had known each other for many years, but Beckett, quel grand homme, a saint, the old man was very proud of his complete collection of signed first editions, The reading of Beckett's work, he told me one day, was as crucial an experience for me, as important in my life, as having survived the concentration camps, by extension, he meant

our being at La Closerie des Lilas that day was, in fact, a kind of sentimental pilgrimage, we were reminiscing about the old man, and that's when Moinous said, C'était le coup de foudre, you know the sort of thing that happens only once in a lifetime, the sort of love affair most of us fantasize about in the long hours we lie awake at night, but which never actually becomes a reality

she walked into his life as though he were a script, a movie script, to play a part, totally unrehearsed, the perfect actress, at ease and self-assured, and what a role she played, she was such a fine actress, she slipped right into the role that was demanded of her, not the real June of course, the fictitious June, the public myth we all admire and desire, though she did say afterwards, as if to confirm the reality of the experience, A man is like an abyss, you get dizzy looking in

as they were running in the streets of Buffalo, away from the ugly demonstration and police brutality, away from the tear gas and the clubbing, June asked, What now, she looked intense, her face mischievously flushed like that of a little girl

I don't know and I don't really give a damn, replied the old guy who was of course much younger then, and quite handsome, well-built and swift, a most appealing figure, secure in his physical stature, solidly muscular because of the tennis and the golf about which he was a fanatic all his life, I did mention that earlier, didn't I, and also because of the swimming, this is not generally known but he had great aquatic talents, almost made it to the 1936 Olympics, in Berlin, as a backstroke specialist, a matter of a tenth of a second, that would have been some encounter with Hitler, another Jesse Owens incident perhaps, he might have been the first Jew ever to win five or six gold medals

he had elegant, refined manners, had he lived in the 17th century, and I wouldn't be surprised if he did, now reincarnated in our century, that old man of ours believed in reincarnation, within reason, he would certainly have been a nobleman, at least a Marquis, yes I can picture him now as a daring flamboyant musketeer of the great Cardinal Richelieu, or better yet, imagine him as the poet laureate at the court of Louis XIV with Racine and La Fontaine, the king's protégé, declaiming sophisticated verse that would ravish the consciousness of his contemporaries, such as, Outside the moon tiptoed across the roofs of our palaces to denounce the beginning of our excessiveness backtracked into the fragility of our decadent adventure, or something like that, incisive and powerful

he had strong features, especially the nose, a topographical sort of nose, a reckless face with lines that were distinct but not precise as though they had been sculptured with an unsharpened chisel, unruly dark brown hair that rose straight up from his forehead with just a touch of gray at the temples, his eyebrows curved like the new moon, his eyes were narrow, disrespectful and amused, revealing a cunning malicious intelligence, his face a combination of pride and humility, effrontery and generosity, his mouth would break into a disarming smile for no specific reason, he had a deep voice, yes of course with a marked French accent, his words were once described by Moinous as tasting like crème caramel, look I'm only reporting here, secondhand, as faithfully as I can, when he spoke, a deliberate misleading humor expressed itself in a maddening prolix pseudologic, the many years he had spent in America seemed to have instilled in him a certain boyishness, a permanent adolescent candor and gaiety, and a love of plain talk, that's how he was, how he looked at the time of his love affair with June Fanon, he was very changeable you know, unpredictable both in his appearance and in his actions, raw energy in constant motion, but always kind and obliging, quite a human being

You seem to be an interesting person, quite a character, June said looking into his face as they stopped a moment to catch their breath, I think I'm going to like you

he put his arm around her shoulders and squeezed her gently to show his appreciation, and his affection too, the kind most liberal Americans had for June Fanon in those troubled days, You're not so bad yourself, he said with a mixture of irony and tenderness in his voice, yes rather fascinating, you would make a great character in a novel

Oh I'm p-paralyzed with happiness to hear you say that, but you know I've been told that before, she smiled knowingly, Daisy-like, obviously echoing a line from a movie or a novel, she was shivering in her mini-skirt though she did have a heavy fur coat thrown casually over her shoulders

Are you cold, he asked

No it's okay, I'm all right

in the distance they could still hear the shouting of the mob and the bursting of the tear gas bombs, What do you say we pursue this adventure a bit further, June said with a sincere look on her face, Hard to tell if she meant it or if she was pretending, Moinous threw that in, but she did look convincing, and so beautiful, so sensually attractive

Fine with me, the old man answered obviously intrigued, and who wouldn't be in a similar situation, our old man was not the type to hesitate, indeed more like him to jump in the water without finding out first if it is too hot or too cold, but one truth is just as good as another, the old man used to say when confronted with a quick decision, how do we know what is more true than anything else, to swim is true, to drown is true, we would nod in approval whenever he'd say that though never quite certain of what he really meant

What did you say, June asked holding on to his arm as they started running again

Oh nothing, I was just mumbling to myself, happily, about the curious way life vibrates in a twofold manner

Hmm, do you often do that, I mean mumble to yourself

just then a cab drove by, the old guy put two fingers in his mouth and let out a loud whistle, something he had learned when he was a kid playing à cache-cache in the streets of Paris, You must have been a boy scout in your youth, June said teasingly, Are you kidding, not me, I've never been a member of anything, no it just came natural, and you should hear me play the saxophone

You play the saxophone

Used to could, as they say in Texas, tenor sax

the cab skidded to a stop on the icy pavement, remember it was a cold dreary winter day in Buffalo, and on top of that it was starting to snow like hell, not that this adds much to the local color but it does give a touch of realism to the situation, Where to, the cabbie asked as he flung open the door of the taxi, you folks look like you're freezing your, your peanuts out there

Speak for yourself Mister, June said as she cuddled next to our old man

Oops, Sorry Lady

Don't mention it, I'm used to it

the old guy looked at June inquiringly, she put her index finger on her mouth, she was thinking, Hey why don't we fly to L.A. first so I can pack a few things and then we can decide where to go, doesn't matter where as long as we are together

How about the Côte d'Azur, the old man suggested bluntly, perhaps it was the wrong place to propose at a time like this, the world situation being as it were somewhat of a mess, the war in Vietnam, crooked politics all over, crises everywhere, the youth rebelling against the establishment and parental authority, prejudice and racism on the rise, but he hadn't been there in years and in the back of his mind he visualized the swanky Monte Carlo casino where he had had a fantastic streak at the roulette wheel on his last visit

Sounds great, what a superb idea, June exclaimed, to the airport cabbie, and let's forget about the revolution, it can wait

You don't mean that, the old man said, I know how committed you are, how involved with politics and human rights

well, I suppose you're right, her face became intense again, but I've been taking so much crap lately, especially from the Hollywood crowd, you know the Bob Hopes John Waynes and company, all those rah-rah Americans, What is she trying to prove, they say I'm discrediting my profession, yes they can speak, meanwhile they bury their heads inside their dollar bills like fat ostriches, well that's their business, maybe they know what they stand for, as for myself, I have to find out who I am, and how I fit into this screwy world of ours, and I don't mean only as a person but as a woman too, you can't spend your life being an image

I understand, he said, he hesitated, maybe we should go back to Lafayette Square and confront the revolution

No, it can wait, she said smiling again and reaching for his hand, you know throwing stones at the cops may not be the best way to solve the problems of this world, feels good when you hit one of them right between the eyes, but then what, perhaps we're not ready yet for the revolution, not ready yet for political reality

Yes I suppose it can wait, agreed the old man, it can wait until we have grown up, politically, until we are ready for the revolution, and anyway most of us live our politics in the past

Or in the future, June added

Yes always in retrospect or in procrastination, always in the if only, if only, the if of what we could have done or will do, if if

Are you two folks some kind of famous political figures, the cabbie asked over his shoulder while glancing at them in his rear view mirror, he had evidently not recognized June Fanon

Not really, you could say we are concerned citizens, that's all

Why all the fireworks out there, the cabbie asked as he veered onto the Kensington Expressway, what are they celebrating, isn't it a bit too early for the 4th of July

You're damn right buddy, June said, it's too early for Independence Day, what you're hearing out there is America cracking at the joints

Oh, that's what it is, puzzled the cabbie

by now they had reached the Buffalo International Airport, June went ahead to check the schedule of departures, Well have a good trip and keep out of trouble, the taxi driver said to the old man who was counting the change, Euh, excuse me Sir, but tell me, the cabbie hesitated, I don't mean to pry Sir, but who is that gorgeous woman you're with, I think I've seen her somewhere before, I mean, she looks familiar, you know what I mean, the old man didn't answer, he simply shrugged off the question, and besides he had just realized that he had given the cabbie his last twenty dollar bill, Oh shit

I've got a problem, he told June when he caught up with her at the airline counter

What's wrong, she asked, you changed your mind

No, it's just that I'm broke, I mean I've got less than twenty bucks on me, that's not going to get us very far, our old man was the most impractical person when it came to money, totally careless, irresponsible, no sense of where money came from and where it went, when there was no more he would simply borrow, hock his watch, his overcoat, all his possessions, Hell with it, but right now there was no time to borrow, not even from us, a direct flight to Los Angeles was leaving in fifteen minutes and they were already boarding the plane, how convenient

Oh that doesn't matter, June said offhandedly with her warm seductive smile, never mind, I've got plenty of money and dozens of credit cards, you'll owe me

on the plane, first class of course, they behaved like young lovers who have just eloped, talked on and on in a whisper, giggled, touched each other searchingly, fondled each other with spontaneous tenderness, letting their mutual desire flow unabashedly, the section where they sat was empty, he told her how he fell in love with her, years ago, When I saw you play that touching, that disturbing part in They Dance through the Night, Oh you saw it, Yes six times, maybe more, What did you think, You were perfect, so real, uncompromising, and tough too, You mean that, Yes of course I do, you were beautifully insolent

You know it's one of my favorite roles, I mean of all the roles I played, one of the most difficult, most demanding I ever had to do, more so even than that of Dolly Pyle, yes when I played Dolly in Caring Love, and let me tell you that was not an easy part to play

Hey, wait a minute, he interrupted her, that's later, I mean it hasn't happened yet, the film hasn't been made yet

So what's the difference, it will happen, the film will be made in
the near future, that's inevitable, don't you know that, somebody eventually has to make that film, so why can't we talk
about it, don't tell me you're that logical, that uptight about
chronology, what do you want me to do, speak in the future
tense, okay, when I play Dolly Pyle in Caring Love I'll know
who I'll be and what I'll want to do, but in They Dance through
the Night I was searching, I was learning you might say,
learning about pain, about suffering, about being used, how
naive I was, you know it's not easy to maintain that kind of
arrogance, that kind of bitchiness, even in a movie, no it's not
easy to sustain that kind of desperate attitude, in a world where
only men have a right to their silent romantic agony, women
somehow are supposed to cry out their inner weaknesses, that's
a lot of crap of course, but that's what I learned in that film, in a
way I think it's when I played Martha in that marathon dance
that I found myself, that was her name, wasn't it, Martha

for an instant her face turned hard and distant as if she was
trying to recapture the depth and the pain of that role, he took
her hand in his, Yes I suppose we are the sum of the roles we
play, those we played in the past and those still to be played in
the future, he said, I don't think he meant to sound that
pompous, that corny, Namredef interjected, but he must have
been trying to impress her

I liked the mixture of toughness and despair you portrayed in
that role, he went on, and without any sentimentality, totally in
control, even when you went into, oh what's his name, Guy
Yeats, Guy Yeats's office to give yourself, or to screw him
rather and put him in his place, wow that was such a fantastic
scene

How nice of you to say that

No I mean it, you were magnificently arrogant, but you know,
deep inside, I think you're very soft, sentimental, vulnerable
even

You may be right, yes vulnerable, perhaps that's why I could not shoot myself at the end and asked Ronnie to do it for me

No I don't mean in the movie, I mean here, here in the real world

Oh what's the damn difference, real life, real world, the movies, fiction, don't you think our being here is like being in a movie, this is totally irrational, look at the two of us sitting here, who is going to believe it, there is something illogical about it

Yes, that's for damn sure, they were silent for a moment, in his mind an inner voice quoted his favorite lines from A Midsummer-Night's Dream, how mawkish can a guy be, Lovers and madmen have such seething brains, such shaping fantasies, that apprehend more than cool reason ever comprehends, the lunatic, the lover, and the poet are of imagination all compact

What are you thinking, she asked, How superb you are, he said in a whisper, and your mouth, ah your mouth especially, he leaned over and kissed her on that beautiful triangular mouth of hers, kissed her softly, and then looked intensely into her eyes, You are a magnificent myth, she laughed throwing her head backward casually, but there was sadness in her pastel green eyes, Ah yes, yes the ignominious search for self-knowledge, isn't that what it's all about, in real life or on the screen, she seemed to be speaking to herself now, and for an instant she became quite inscrutable, but then her hand reached for his face and she touched him, touched his eyes, his mouth, pinched his cheek gently, You're quite a man, and a real charmer too, she added snapping out of her mood into that mischievous little girl smile so typical of her, he didn't answer at first, but then, half-joking half-serious, No I think of myself more as a seedy solipsist

Well well, you don't say, what conceit, you must be some kind of literary man, a seedy solipsist, I'll be damned, like Murphy, how appropriate, he blushed, June could not know of course how fond our old man was of echoing plagiaristically those self-indulgent words of that burlesque irrational figure of modern fiction who was introduced into the world of literature, you may recall, Moinous was speaking now, under the motto, Amor intellectualis quo Murphy se ipsum amat, a motto which could aptly define our old man too under a different set of circumstances

A seedy solipsist, how incredibly funny, June burst into laughter, that makes one wonder what the hell you're doing here with me, doesn't it, no Sir you seem too extrovert, too youthful and spontaneous to speak like this, she passed her fingers playfully through his wiry hair

Don't let the appearance fool you, I am ageless, or rather I should say I merely endure my atavistic assumptions

Oh you weird egghead, if you go on like this we might land on another planet, she was being facetious of course, but little did she know how prophetic her remark was, June Fanon was deported to the space colonies in 1997

it was a grim sad day, that new year's eve 1997, when June and thousands of other world citizens were deported to the space colonies, our old man found out quite by chance, while reading a recent copy of the Annual Solar System Gazette in the waiting room of his dentist, he had a terrible toothache that day, and that's where he came across the list of the deportees for that year, just the names, no reasons given as usual, he was glancing at the list when he saw her name, Fanon June, sandwiched in alphabetical order between the names Fancy Simon and Fonderman Marguerite, his throat tightened for a moment, many years had passed since those memorable days, those fleeting passionate weeks they had spent together, he even wept a little, I think, while holding on to his jaw which was hurting like hell, wrinkled old geezer in pain as yet unaware of his own fate

but this was years later, right now, on the plane to California, they were silent again, his hand resting on her thigh, her head on his shoulder, and then slowly, serenely, they both fell asleep exhausted after the intense and unexpected events of the day as the jet flew over the Grand Canyon and on to California, and its lemon sun, that 's how Namredef and Moinous recounted the beginning of this adventure, at La Closerie des Lilas, as the three of us ordered another round of Pernod with water

Namredef and Moinous have a disorienting way of talking at the same time, interrupting each other, which makes it difficult to keep their stories straight, especially the chronology, sometimes one of them starts relating something, begins to articulate a sentence, and right in the middle of it the other will take over, as if they were of one mind, one mouth, often wandering into endless digressions, surprising detours and circumvolutions, in English, in French, doesn't matter, they are both bilingual, they weave in and out of words as though language for them were a rumor transmissible ad infinitum in any direction, that's how they function, how close, how inseparable they are, two voices within a single voice interloping, it's maddening, but after a while one gets used to their way of speaking, and in any event I doubt I can go on without them, bring this project to a satisfactory conclusion without their help and their wisdom

no I'm sure I can't, and besides in this lonely business of ours one does not choose one's collaborators, melancholic or rambunctious as they may be, they simply appear, usually in the middle of the night, the middle of a sleepless night, and you're stuck with them

IV

We were still sitting at La Closerie des Lilas, Namredef, Moinous, and I, and were just beginning to attack the first course of what turned out to be a most sumptuous meal, Namredef and Moinous had ordered escargots de Bourgogne, and I was enjoying a terrine de pâté maison, it may have been selfish on our part to indulge like this while the old man sat alone and resigned in his antechamber of departure, but what else could we do, we had tried everything so far, and still hadn't been able to come up with anything tangible about his deportation, all our investigations had led nowhere, all our questions to the authorities had produced only evasive answers, and time was running out

taking turns between mouthfuls, Namredef and Moinous went on relating the old man's love affair with June Fanon, for since all else had proved futile, it became evident to us that it was perhaps in the details of the old man's life, however insignificant, that we might stumble on the clue that would lead us to an understanding of his present predicament

from Los Angeles they flew directly to the Riviera, Moinous picked up the narrative, to Nice, and there were seen in every casino from Menton to San Tropez, June turned out to be as mad a gambler, as reckless as he was, and were they lucky, you won't believe it, Moinous said excitedly, obviously delighted for his old friend who was not always that lucky, that's for sure, winning huge sums at the roulette table, playing by intuition, indifferent to the odds, no system, imagine that

they stood close to each other at the side of the wheel staring defiantly at the little white bouncing ball, composing strange combinations of numbers in their minds, their hands full of chips, big ones, Number five, cover the fives, she said, and he placed a pile of chips on the five, fifteen, twenty-five, thirty-five, without hesitation, casually, almost arrogantly, I'm sure it's going to be one of the fives, she whispered to him, the little ball took a final leap, Cinq Rouge Impair et Manque, the croupier shouted as if happy for them, and our friend shoved another pile of chips in his pockets

Seventeen now, play the seventeen this time, I can feel it, June was all excited, Rien ne va plus, she squeezed his arm hard as the croupier spun the ball around the wheel, and unbelievably, Dix-sept Noir Impair et Manque, they were on a streak, no doubt about it, even the croupiers seemed to be enjoying the moment, everyone was looking at them in astonishment, Finale trois maintenant, vas-y mon vieux, June was fluent in his native tongue, with a delicious accent, let it ride on all the threes, Are you sure, he asked while covering the threes, Trust me, I know what I'm doing, Faites vos jeux Mesdames et Messieurs, he doubled the mise, and twenty-three it was, how amazing

Quick cover the five again, triple the bets, June was calling all the shots, they couldn't miss, people were pushing and shoving around the table, greedy fingers reaching between their hands to follow every one of their lucky moves, June, of course, tried to be incognito, but even with her dark glasses and the bleached blond wig they bought together for the occasion, as a joke, people recognized her, Oh look, it's June Fanon, Isn't she gorgeous, Ah go on, don't be shy, ask her for an autograph, Mais si vas-y quoi sois pas timide, dis-lui que tu la trouves formidable, No I have no idea who the guy with her is, must be a friend, Or maybe a film director, Or a producer, Non non je suis sûr que c'est pas Midas, moi je le connais Midas, But this guy is damn good-looking too, I bet you he's her secret lover

all she had to do was smile or speak a few words with her All-American voice and a crowd would gather, her loose fawn-like gestures gave her away, It's the way you move, the way you float, it's inevitable, he told her, there is something unreal, something mystical about you, and yet you're so real, you're just perfect

Stop it, you exaggerate, I feel so inadequate at times, so mis-placed, sometimes I think I'm only what people imagine, trans-fixed into a lifeless image, they were standing by the sea in Monte Carlo and she was gazing intently into the water, he put his arms around her and her mouth reached eagerly for his, he touched her breasts, then let his hand slide down along her hip, she was wearing a silky black dress and he felt her flesh through the thin material, she pressed her thighs against his with aban-don, behind them Monte Carlo was whirling indifferently with the winners and the losers, Moinous inserted that remark in his narrative as he went on recounting what the old man had told my two narrators about his love affair with June Fanon

it was hard to concentrate on the words she was speaking now, between her voice and the sound of the waves something kept sending me back, yes her voice especially with its subliminal pull, into old movies and faded dreams, her reflection becoming mine, You know you are even more beautiful in reality than you appear on the screen, I told her

she turned her face away, stepped to the edge of the sea, picked up a pebble and threw it in the water fragmenting the moon, It's because screen images are ultimately devoid of life, she said, life is what matters, yes that's what makes people pretty, she took my hand and pulled me gently away, Come let's go back to the hotel

in our room that night, after we celebrated our incredible streak of luck, giggling and laughing while drinking a bottle of cham-

pagne, we made love, at first in a kind of frenzy, moving
enlaced from the table to the floor, standing in front of the
mirror, and finally falling onto the bed where June suddenly
said to me, You know I have never spoken to anyone before the
way I speak to you, with you I feel free, yes full of abandon, she
sat up and threw herself over me, hugging and kissing my face
all over, we made love again, not frantically this time, gently,
playfully, her body was softer than I had imagined, but nervous and vibrant, responsive, it made me feel kind and generous, I held her by the back of the head with one hand while my
other hand lifted her hips toward me, her legs squeezed my
body tightly, she was caressing my back, running her nails
along my spine, our bodies were moving in unison, but there
was no moaning, no sighing, just quiet pleasure

Yes with you I feel fulfilled, we were resting next to each other
on the bed, one of her legs crossed over mine, Maybe it's
because we are crowding so much into these few moments, I
explained

that's the best he could say, remarked Moinous, not brilliant for
a man of letters, but I suppose it's not always easy to avoid
banalities, and besides he was feeling sentimental that night

It's also a matter of surviving, images change, she said as if
reconnecting with our earlier conversation by the sea, but being
with you seems to make things more permanent, and so comfortable, being with you is like wearing a pair of old sneakers,
you know beat-up old sneakers one never wants to throw away

she had a quizzical expression on her face, I hugged her, and
again we made love, slowly, hardly moving our bodies, and it
felt as though I was watching myself make love to her in a
dream, her skin was smooth, perfumed, her thighs firm, her
nipples hard, it was almost morning, the light beginning to
filter through the drawn curtains, Are we dreaming this whole
thing, I asked as I passed my hand over her face

No it's not a dream, she pinched my behind hard, Aiie, that
hurts, why did you do that, To prove to you that you're not

asleep, she moved closer and rested her head on my chest, We screw well together eh, she said, we're so nice together

Pas mal, mais c'est parce que tu m'inspires, ou plutôt disons que c'est en hommage à June que nous nous surpassons

Hey don't pull that French stuff on me mister, she said jumping out of bed while throwing the blankets over my face, she stood naked in front of the mirror and started doing body exercises

You're beautiful, I was watching her from the bed, my hands crossed behind my head propped on the pillow

suddenly she turned toward me, Maybe you're right, yes maybe we are dreaming this whole thing, but then what's the difference, how do I know when I am real or simply a fictitious character in a story, after a while in my kind of life one loses one's perspective on reality, I'm never sure who I am and where I am

That sounds like something out of one of those avant-garde novels, I said, but I'll tell you something, my dear June, right now you're quite real, and so beautiful

But you, you, who are you, I mean tell me about you, I know so little about your life, she had a talent for making him reveal himself, they had left the Riviera and were driving to Lake Como in a rented car, a blue Alfa Romeo, Moinous specified

he was staring at the road, My life began in a closet, he said giving his voice an affected eloquence as if playing the lead in an old-fashioned melodrama, Among empty skins and dusty hats, while sucking pieces of stolen sugar

Why are you joking

I'm not joking, I'm serious, it's from a poem, an old poem I wrote a long time ago which recalled my days among the beasts

Go on, it's beautiful, I want to hear more

No, it doesn't work any more, it's all wrong

What do you mean it doesn't work, do poems work and then they don't work any more

Yes sometimes they do sometimes they don't, like movies, they get old, they lose their meaning, their potency

Then tell me something about you that works

he hesitated, concentrating on the narrow road which was winding through the mountains alongside a steep precipice, I am a survivor, my death is behind me

Phew, why the morbidity suddenly when we're so happy together

I'm not morbid, I'm happy, can't you see, yes happy to be here with you, but you see the fact of being a survivor, of living with one's death behind, in a way makes you free, free and irresponsible toward your own end, of course you feel a little guilty while you're surviving because there is this thing about your past, your dead past and all that, but you have to get on with things, sustain your excessiveness, so to speak, yes imagine you have this wretched past, so wretched, gruesome, but it's the only past you've got, I mean you're stuck with it, but then they take it away from you, erase it, make typographical symbols out of it, funny little xxxx's on pieces of paper, you're dead as far as they are concerned, nonexistent, I mean how do you live without a past, well you manage to survive anyhow, to fake it, fictitiously, extemporaneously, not as revenant but as a devenant, by projecting yourself ahead of yourself

June looked puzzled, I don't think I follow you, you're too vague, can't you be more specific, I mean what good are all these abstractions, but go on it's interesting, and I like to listen to you talk, you have a sexy accent when you speak English

a sign on the road said Lago di Como 32 kms, We're almost there, he said, and then went on, Well you invent yourself as you go along, re-invent what you think really happened, this way you can survive anything, survive a precipice, like this one, he pointed to the side of the road and the car swerved toward the precipice

Hey watch out, I'm not ready for my end yet, June cried out

Don't worry, everything is under control, he smiled as the tires screeched on the curve, Yes you can survive anything, a parachute jump, a winter of starvation, a war, a concentration camp, even a disastrous love affair, survive anything, it's a matter of stubbornness, but do you bring up that dead past afterward, no, you simply allow it to be, how shall I say, to be the central unspeakable event that charges your life and your work emotionally, but without going into the sordid details

Hmm, I think I get the sense of what you're taking about, June said, but still it's debatable, there is something wrong in what you say, something inconsistent, somehow I feel that you are refusing to tell me the real experience behind all that, but if I understand what you are trying to say, or not say, you have found a way to make your past live by pointing to its grave with your finger and of course we can't catch you at it, it's just a motion, a gesture, a clever substitution, and this way you put all your guilt on others, on us, but the fact that you choose to speak about it, even evasively, and write about it too, I suppose, is that transcendence or escape

Yes that's exactly the problem, exactly what my life is all about, transcendence or escape, you've put your finger right on it, though I would say more escaping than transcending, perhaps if you and I had met sooner you would have helped me transcend rather than escape

they remained silent for a long time, they had arrived in Lake Como, the place seemed dead, it was raining, they drove around through the narrow deserted streets, past the Bellagio Promontory, the Porta Vittoria, the Santa Maria Maggiore Cathedral, the splendid Palazzo Rusconi, stopped a moment to admire the monument to Alessandro Manzoni, Not a bad novelist you know, the old man said, a bit too romantic for my taste, but not to be scorned, then they crossed the Piazza Cavour to the lakeshore drive, Beautiful place but not very lively, June remarked, yes it's rather dull, the old man retorted, we may be out of luck, I bet you the casino is closed, and indeed Como looked like a ghost town at this time of year with most of its elegant hotels closed for the season and its seedy private villas all shuttered

Let's stay in this town for a few days, June said, it's so empty, so decadent, it's perfect for us

Do you know, the old man asked, as they were registering at the Albergo Carramaza, one of the few hotels they found open, what the title of the poem I started to quote before is

No, I have no idea

Escape, it's called Escape

Oh that's interesting, will you read it to me later

I don't have a copy with me but perhaps I can recite it to you from memory

the lady behind the desk said to them in French after she looked over the registration card where he had signed Monsieur et Madame Onsenfout, Eh bien j'espère que vous vous plairez ici, c'est si tranquille vous savez à cette époque, she gestured toward the empty lobby where, in one corner, two old men were quietly playing dominoes, while in front of the picture window an elegant old lady was doing her knitting next to a dozing gentleman whose legs were wrapped in a blanket

Charming place, June said

Don't you like it

Oh I love it

they were sitting on the veranda of the hotel now, overlooking the lake, it had stopped raining but the sky was gray, and the lake gray too, they had ordered a bottle of Lombardy wine, he looked past her face as though reading the text of his poem against the landscape, My life began in a closet among empty skins and dusty hats while sucking pieces of stolen sugar, outside the moon tiptoed across the roof to denounce the beginning of my excessiveness backtracked into, no wait, wait, that's not it, ah damn I forgot how it goes, backtracked into, hell, into, oh I got it, into the fragility of my adventure, curiosity drove me down the staircase but I slipped on the twelfth step and fell and all the doors opened dumb eyes to stare at my nakedness, as I ran beneath the sky, yes that's how it goes I think, as I ran beneath the sky a yellow star struck my chest and all the eyes turned away, then they grabbed me and locked me in a box, rolled me a hundred times over the earth in metaphorical disgrace while they chased each other with stones in their hands and burned all the stars in a furnace, every day they came to touch me, to put their fingers in my mouth and paint me black and blue, but through a crack in the wall I saw a tree the shape of a leaf, and one morning a bird flew into my head, I loved that bird so much that while my blue-eyed master looked at the sun and was blind, I opened the cage and hid my heart in a yellow feather, he took a sip of wine from his glass, Yes I think that's how it ends, and hid my heart in a yellow feather, that's the story

How beautiful, and it's so moving, I think I understand now what you meant before about surviving

No it's sentimental, and too hermetic

I don't agree with you, I like it, it works, and besides it tells me a great deal about you

we were still at La Closerie des Lilas, on our third or fourth course, when Namredef interrupted Moinous, Oh that's just what I feel like, a good bottle of Lombardy wine, Hé garçon, une bouteille de vin de Lombardie, s'il vous plaît, du blanc

Toute de suite, Monsieur

By the way, Namredef said to me, did you know that our old man had been in Como before

No, I didn't know that, when

With his wife, just after they were married, she's the one who told us when we finally spoke to her

You spoke to her

Oh we forgot to tell you, yes we finally located her, only a few weeks ago, in Vienna, where she was born in fact

Yes I knew that, I mean that she was born in Vienna, but I didn't know she had gone back there

Sure, she went back to Vienna in 1990, immediately after they were separated, you know, the Dismarital Law, she said it was too difficult, too painful for her to be so close to him in America and yet not be able to care for him, and you know what, she had no idea about his deportation, she hadn't heard a thing about it, of course she wanted to come back with us at once to try and do something, I'll go with him if necessary, she even said, but we told her it wouldn't do any good, that perhaps it was already too late, and besides it would have been too exhausting for her, and too disturbing, she's very old now

but what a lovely woman, Moinous cut in, yes quite old, like him, but still in full control of her senses, well, more or less, and still very beautiful, no she didn't give us any clues, nothing whatsoever, as Nam told you, she didn't even know about it, I mean the deportation, and I don't think she realizes what it means, she lives very much alone with her memories, she just talked about their life together, especially that period just after they were married and took that crazy trip through Europe, the two of us, a kind of honeymoon, though frankly we could not afford it then, but he was like that, so careless with money, we gambled everywhere, our common vice, we were so wild in those days, ah yes what a trip, a long series of jumps from casino to casino, winning one night, losing the next, sometimes losing more than we could afford, we kept cashing checks at the American Express which were not even covered, but we didn't care, and I was just as irresponsible as he was, I remember, we spent a few days in Lake Como, what a charming place, it was during the winter, the town was deserted, we were still discovering each other at the time, and so in love, he had just started writing a novel, he would work all morning in our room at the hotel while I sat in a lounge chair on the veranda, reading, then he would come down and read me the pages he had just written, it was a strange sad book, there was no story, or rather the story was all pulverized, as if it refused to be told, the story of a little boy who had been locked in a closet, but it was hard to follow, I kept saying to him, Why don't you tell the story straight and stop playing games, but he would get angry, You don't understand a damn thing, it's not the story that counts, it's the way you tell it, he was so stubborn, so uncompromising, and yet, somehow, I knew he had to write it this way, he had to, I suppose I was the only one who understood that

from Lake Como we went south, yes I remember, by train, to Florence, just to visit the Galleria Degli Uffizi, to see the Botticellis, I've always been fond of Botticelli, he used to say to me, It's because you look like his women, ethereal and voluptuous, he was exaggerating of course, teasing me, we rushed from room to room in that immense dusty museum, up and down those marble staircases, we must have looked like typical tourists, bumping into people, stopping here and there to admire a great painting or a sculpture, he was full of knowledge about painting, he would lecture to me in front of each tableau, but I didn't mind, he always had something fascinating to say, even if most of the time he was merely inventing, he often said if he had to do it all over again he would be a painter, like his father, did you know that his father was an artist, a surrealist painter, yes before, before he was exterminated, his father, I never knew him, but I understand he was a remarkable man, not very lucky though, but my poor husband, he couldn't draw a straight line, or knock a nail in the wall without demolishing it, couldn't do anything with his hands, I've never known anyone so clumsy with his hands

it's quite a place that Galleria, have you ever been there, though I recall he said, I really don't like this place, it's like a supermarket of art, a flea market, everything in here is shoved together, he was right, nothing really works together there, all these paintings and sculptures seem misplaced, I remember we stopped for a long time at the top of a huge staircase to look at Donatello's wooden statue of Mary Magdalen, and I said, What simplicity, look how her hands are not quite clasped, and yet clearly prayer is her only hope, and he replied, somewhat annoyed, Yes but the way she's placed here, on this pedestal, squared off from the viewer by this railing, the intimacy of her gesture is dissolved and replaced by the worship we're supposed to feel for art, that's what's wrong with this place, it makes us passive worshipers rather than allowing us to be compassionate witnesses, It's true, I said, you're right, I hadn't noticed, but still she's beautiful, don't you think

I don't know why I still remember this conversation so vividly, somehow it stayed with me all these years, perhaps because it shows how different we were, and yet how we complemented each other, and yes I remember now, just then an old man stopped next to us, I can still see his wrinkled face, his cunning gray eyes, I suppose he must have heard what we were saying because he said to us, She doesn't care, she's not looking at us, see how her eyes are averted toward the dismal past or the uncertain future, and then he walked away, that old man, just like that, I wish we could have talked to him some more, maybe he was an artist, or a guide, he had a name tag on his coat, yes in fact I never forgot the name, Minkoff, that's what it was, Minkoff, he was not an American, he had an accent, but his English was almost perfect, it's strange how sometimes a quick apparition like this stays with you for the rest of your life, I can still see his face, I suppose that's how my dear husband must look now, it's been ten years, yes ten years since I last saw him

then we went on to Rome, it was as though we were running

away from something, from the rest of the world, in any
direction, searching frantically for some ideal place to be alone,
and yet always ending up in the most crowded places as if
subconsciously we wanted to be seen together, to have people
notice how happy we were, it must have shown on our faces,
and all the while we kept on talking, about anything, everything, in the Vatican Museum of Modern Art we stood for a
moment in front of a Chagall dedicated to Pope John, How
curious, I said, that a Jew should dedicate his work to the Pope,
my husband didn't answer at first, but after a while he said, I
like his work less and less, it's sentimental, too easy, it's for
those who still believe, I suppose that's why he gave it to the
Pope, we moved on, we were still at the stage of discovering
each other, who we were, what we felt and thought, and it came
out in bits and pieces, few words here, few words there, I
suppose it's always like this when you're first married, yes I
remember, later that day we were standing in the middle of the
Coliseum, stray cats were rubbing at our feet, there were so
many of them and they looked like they were starving, it scared
me, and suddenly, quite unexpectedly, he said to me, I've been
called a futilitarian, that's what he said, just like that, I still
don't know why, he sounded sad now, I wander here and there,
from place to place, most of the time inside my head, There are
lots of people like that, I told him, Yes I know, lots of people
like us who look at the world but the world doesn't look back,
that's what's tragic about life, we were facing each other, he
held me by the shoulders and looked into my eyes, But right
now, right here you and I are looking at each other, aren't we, I
said, and the world is looking at us, isn't it, Yes, yes, his face
became joyful, and that's why we exist

after that we flew to Athens, it was crazy, we hadn't planned on
going there, we saw a poster somewhere that showed Athens,
and we left, there was a mad frenzy in our need to go on, to
move to yet another place, to keep talking endlessly, though
sometimes we remained silent for long stretches of time, lying
in bed next to each other, touching one another, and after a
while I'd ask, What are you thinking about, it seemed that a
phrase kept running through his mind, in French for some
reason, I don't know why, though it's true we often spoke

French together, and besides his whole life was a mishmash of French and English, in his thinking as well as in his writing, as if he wanted the two languages to merge inside of him, but that day when I asked him what he was thinking he answered, La vérité de ce monde c'est la mort, il faut choisir, mourir ou mentir, I looked at him puzzled and said, Tu sais cela ne me dit pas grand chose sur notre situation présente, she has a delightful accent when she speaks French, Moinous said, And besides I don't want to die and I don't want to lie either, I tried to laugh when I said that, Tu ne comprends pas que mourir et aimer c'est la même chose, he replied as he held me against him

that was so long ago, he was not an easy man to understand, so moody at times, and yet so full of life too, so exuberant, but what contradictions in him, he once said to me when we lived in Santa Barbara, America does not exist, I know, I live there, that's how he was, thirty years, yes thirty years we lived together, shared everything, and still I never knew what went on inside of him, something huge that obsessed him all the time

from Athens we went to the Island of Corfu, we were walking in the narrow streets of the Old Quarter, I remember, I was wearing the big straw hat he bought me in one of the little shops, we were angry, angry at ourselves and at each other, we had just lost all our money at the casino, all of it, at that sumptuous but decadent palace which Princess Elizabeth of Austria built on top of a hill and where you gamble on a terrace, with soft music, everything we had lost, and he wanted to turn in our plane tickets back to the States, get a refund, he kept insisting, I tell you with that money we can win everything back

sell the tickets, I was not that crazy, I said No, never, and he knew I meant it, oh was I in a rage, can you imagine that, the idea of wanting to sell those tickets

You look like a tigress when you're angry, he said to me, come you wild beast let's go back to the hotel and make love, Damn you, I cried, and how are we going to pay for that hotel, Ah we'll sneak out of there, he said, and we did, without paying, through one of the side doors, I was so scared, but he was like that, and I was getting used to his erratic behavior, his quick way of brushing aside the most disastrous situations, though I could never tell if it hurt him inside or not

I was so angry, I'm not going to listen to you any more, I said, I don't want to hear any more of your mad raving, yes let's go back to the hotel and pack and let's get out of here, and that very afternoon, after we sneaked out through that side door, we flew back to the States, oh were we crazy in those days, but so in love

she sounds like quite a woman, I said when Namredef stopped talking, just the way I remember her

yes quite a woman, Namredef and Moinous nodded their heads, and you cannot imagine how much she still cares for him

but tell me, did she say anything at all about the old man's deportation, why he has been selected

not a word, we told you that already, she didn't even know about it, the only thing she said to us, just as we were leaving, as if trying to give us a message, was to quote something, something we think the old man once wrote, she grasped her forehead with one hand as if trying to remember the exact words, and then she whispered, No I cannot resign myself to being the inventory of his miscalculations, I am not ready for my summation

that's interesting, it's from one of his poems, but doesn't help us much, well that's that, but now tell me what about June and the old man, what happened to them

oh they stayed in Como, they went on talking, making love, having a good time together, Moinous began again

one afternoon they were walking on the promenade by the lake, the sun had finally broken through the clouds, it was a nice day, though a bit cold, he was quiet, thoughtful, Why are you so serious, June asked, I'm not serious, just thinking, About what, he hesitated, you know I didn't tell you but I was in Como before, years ago, with someone I loved very much, and still love, Your wife, Yes my wife, Damn you, why do you have to tell me that, June pulled her arm away from his, I don't know, he said, I really don't know I'm sorry

Oh forget it, I didn't mean to be bitchy, I suppose we all have our little secrets, and our little moments of guilt, she took his arm again, but stop being so serious and say something, anything, talk to me, a person cannot be silent, even when traveling through seas of thoughts there is no interior silence

Yes, you're right, he answered, but then all we can salvage from our passage through adult consciousness is irony or sarcasm

she shook her head, It's amazing how you can go on and on with these naive profundities, she seemed annoyed

No listen to me, he stopped walking and faced her, you see, you and I here, day by day we are shedding our redundancies, when it'll be over we will be new again, that's what I mean by irony

Hey I like that, it's a nice thought, he raised his hand to his mouth, Yes a nice thought but it's only a thought and thoughts never change anything, they just come and go

So what's wrong with that

Nothing, except that thinking is not the worst, what is terrible is to have thought, at times he would just keep on like this, almost irrational in his intellectual fervor, but she stayed right with him, One can say the same of living, or of loving for that matter

Certainly, except that in living we can change, we can modify the results of our actions, which our death will eventually immortalize, transfix forever, but we cannot change anything with thinking even though we pretend to do so, this is why one can never retreat from life, but one can always escape from thought, and yet to have lived is not enough, to have loved is not enough, one must talk about it constantly, he seemed gloomy now, preoccupied, and she didn't know what to say, then he added ponderously, I think I've reached moribundity

Oh damn you, she screamed, you old fool, I don't want to hear any more of that, and then after a long moment of silence June said softly, come let's go back to the hotel and make love

he put his arm around her waist as they walked back to the hotel, suddenly he stopped and pointed to the lake, and to the mountains beyond the lake, The universe is a vast autoerotic ring

Here you go again, she teased, you're incorrigible

but he ignored her, Yes a serpent with its tail in its mouth, it knows no difference between beginning and end

Yes I know I know, she said with a touch of deliberate sarcasm in her voice, it merely vibrates in a twofold manner, you know I'm beginning to worry about you, seriously, if you go on like this one of these days you're going to be shipped to another planet, upside down, and then you'll really be sorry, she laughed and started skipping on one leg like a little girl, yes they'll send you to the moon or even further than that

Hmm, very interesting, he paused, it's the second time since we've been together that you've suggested I be sent to another planet, do you know something I don't

back in their room at the Albergo Carramaza they drank champagne and were both quite high, happily giddy, and then he started ranting again as though following in his mind the blurry lines of some abstract design, There are two forms of failure possible, the failure to possess, which is tragic, and the failure to communicate, which is comic

Well, in this case, June said standing naked in the middle of the room, legs spread apart, arms akimbo, as if parodying herself in the role of Stellababe, either we go on talking nonsense and make comic fools of ourselves, or else we make love immediately and avoid becoming tragic figures

You're magnificent, he said his mouth breaking into a smile as he pulled her gently toward the bed, Why can't we simply be tragicomic

it lasted only a few weeks, four or five at the most, Namredef and Moinous reported, they rushed from place to place, talked on and on, made love at every conceivable time of night and day, and then it was finished, their lives called them back, she to another movie, another role to play, beyond this story, another series of images, he to his fiction, the book he was then writing, or was going to write now

I have to leave in the morning, she announced one evening, nothing more, he didn't flinch, he went on with whatever he was saying at the time as though he had not heard what she had said, he didn't even blink, but later that evening he said to her, I feel like I should thank you for something but I don't know what

Me too, she replied, but I don't know what either, and the following morning she left, he heard her get up early and pack her suitcase but pretended to be asleep, after that he never spoke of her again, never, Moinous and Namredef stopped talking

after a moment of silence I said, And now unless we prevent his departure her memory will go with him to the colonies, unless we do something quickly as he waits in that antechamber, the buzzing in his head will blur the images of his past

Perhaps they will meet again there, Moinous suggested unconvincingly

Yes, but how would we know

we ordered another bottle of wine for the cheese and dessert, then sat for a while in contemplative silence, I wondered what June Fanon would say of the whole situation, or if she remembered him at all

The whole thing sounds like a parody of life, I said finally when we were almost finished eating

Perhaps, Namredef replied while chewing a piece of fromage de chèvre, but there is parody only in relation to an authenticity more or less hidden

Quite right, Moinous added picking up the thread of the conversation, there is caricature only in reference to a non-degraded form, words lie only to those who are haunted by the truth of words

It may be so, I said as I emptied my glass of wine, but meanwhile our old friend is still locked in that room, and what do we do, we talk on and on, we reminisce, we stuff ourselves with good food and philosophize like a bunch of eggheads, how inconsiderate of us

V

Yes, tomorrow I shall be on my way, he told us when we saw him, just a few hours ago, and he still refuses to do anything, say anything to save himself, even though we tried to convince him that some mistake must have been made, After all, we pointed out, computers do register human errors, it's well known

oh you did say that to him

yes of course, we even told him that all our inquiries at the highest level of government have not produced any solid evidence for his deportation, not even vague indications, nothing

and what did he say to that

well, nothing much, just Dear friends, it's too late, leave me, leave me now, I want to be alone for a while, with old Sam

but there is still time, we have not yet exhausted all the possibilities, all the official and nonofficial resources available to us, after all we are still, as you are too, members in good standing of WAO, yes indeed distinguished members of the World Association of the Outspoken, and that certainly counts, please give us a clue, anything, none of the usual reasons, insinuations, the standard blah blahs one hears in cases of misdeportation seem to apply in your case, do help us

No dear Nam, dear Moimoi, it's useless, useless, he said with a touch of cynicism in his voice as he stroked Sam on the head

it's not surprising, I say leaning back in my chair in front of my desk, true cynics are often the kindest people, for they see the hollowness of life, and from the realization of that hollowness is generated a kind of cosmic pity, and so it is here

yes, Moinous confirms, no one has earned his vision more rigorously and more painfully than he has, yet there is no self-pity in him, I can assure you, not a trace

oh I'm sure of that, on the contrary, if I know him the pity goes out to those who decided his fate, unwillingly or mistakenly

but meanwhile we friends, witnesses, old fellow-voices gathered here to orchestrate his exit, his departure, expulsion, dammit, feel so helpless on the threshold of another sad beginning for him, splintered hopelessly as our mutual traces linger along diverging tracks, we don't usually speak that eloquently, that pompously, Namredef and Moinous tell me, but the occasion calls for it

I nod my head in mild agreement, what else can I do, he deserves better in spite of his faults, his egotism, his imperfections, weaknesses, no man is ever perfect, yes in spite of his stubbornness, his lack of reason, his foolish lingering from the primordial closet of his strange birth so many years ago, that unthinkable beginning of mine, as he used to say, to this ultimate box, metallic box here at the gate of the new century, or is it the closing gap, after all the frantic motions, the millions and millions of words and gestures wasted

these are his words, I'm only reporting here, secondhand

What, oh you people would like to know how I manage to obtain all this information, from the narrators of course, Namredef and Moinous, the narrators of this story who will be more clearly identified, more precisely situated in this intramural presentation, as they pursue their investigation, as they report the anxiety, the self-doubt, the fear of our old man, but the joy too, and the laughter, mad radical laughter of his existence, therefore allow us a little elegance, a touch of decorum, style, yes style is called for here, on the outskirts of darkness, that endlessness of survival on the edge of the precipice, leaning against the wind, style for the journey of tomorrow, for if the night passes quietly tomorrow he will be among the expelled, banished from our world, the decision is irreversible, we were told

wrinkled old body undying, sitting in the final closet, the waiting room, the transitory space of his potential future among the stars, and like the many others, men, women, children of all races, also waiting each in their own antechamber of departure, thousands of them, the new year's eve 1999 contingent, already dressed in the traditional white tunic of those marked for the colonies, nice touch, gathering his memories, the remnants of his past, but also premembering, precalling the days, months, years to come in the great void ahead, the great cunt of space, as Moinous once called it in a moment of frustrated anger

if only he would say something, I'm sure he knows the reason, but no, all he told us, Namredef and Moinous continue, a few hours ago when we visited him, as he went on stroking his faithful dog, Words are both what help us get where we want to go and prevent us from getting there, so why speak, it's useless, leave me now for a while, I need to be alone, prepare myself for tomorrow

prepare yourself, shit, how, tell us how, we asked, he didn't sound that formal, that pompous, it's not like him, not at all, on the contrary, always jovial, always carefree, playful, informal, yes always full of subtle ironies, always in good spirits even in the most painful, the most horrendous moments of his life, the most disastrous situations, and let me tell you there were many disastrous moments in his life, and yet how often did we watch him laugh himself back to happiness, back to careless optimism

perhaps that is the reason why he is being sent to the space colonies, I venture to my two narrators, his unshakable optimism, it wouldn't be the first case, many have been deported lately for exhibiting too much optimism, too much hilarity

no, that's what we thought at first, Namredef and Moinous shake their heads, but we were assured otherwise, it would be too ridiculous, his optimism, why not his stubbornness then, or his anal compulsion, no that would be too far-fetched, though it's true that our old man has always been an ardent optimist, and laughter often rescued him from the lower depths of depression, and even once, do you remember Moinous, laughing himself back to health in the middle of a lengthy and almost fatal illness

yes I remember, it was in Sicily, when he had tuberculosis, just like his father, spitting his blood down the toilet bowl, coughing pieces of lung, he had been advised by medical specialists to seek a warm dry climate, or else, not that he could afford it, certainly not, but we helped, and others too, we were inseparable in those days

we were sitting on the balcony of that lovely Pensione di Sole in Palermo, the three of us, do you remember, must be a good fifty years ago, Oh more than that, yes the three of us, like another saintly trinity, we were his Paul Rée and Lou Salomé

he was depressed that day, so depressed, his condition was not improving, You know, he said staring blankly at the sea, I am seriously contemplating suicide just not to witness the eventual failure of my life, but of course that would be another form of delusion, for to leave one's life, one's work unfinished implies the possibility of success, what is left unlived, untold, may contain the potential truth one always seeks, those who kill themselves do so with the conviction that they would have reached that truth eventually had they lived to the proper end, they die in the illusion of hope which in a way keeps the rest of us alive

we didn't say anything to that, coming from him that kind of logic always made us speechless, he had a curious smile on his face

It's not that unusual, I interrupt my narrators, in this world of ours the old aching concern for self-destruction is often mixed with a distant and glittery-eyed glee

Namredef ignores me and goes on relating what happened on that balcony, and then he started telling us a story, not unlike him to burst into stories in the middle of a depression, that strange story he's told so often about the little boy in the closet

The soldiers were already in the courtyard, calling their names, his voice sounded remote, it was early in the morning, very early, six in the morning, in July, I think, or perhaps August, hard to remember, and the mother quietly awoke the boy, he was only twelve then, she was crying softly, shhh, shhh, the boy must be saved, she said as she gently pushed him into a closet, he was wearing his little boy shorts, a closet just outside the door of their apartment, on the landing, on the third floor, it was impossible to tell if the old man was inventing what he was relating or remembering it, a dark box where they stored old clothes, empty skins, dusty hats, he called them, and old newspapers, and after the soldiers took away his mother, his father, and his two sisters, stumbling down the staircase with their bundles, nomad bundles is how he described them, moaning yellow stars on their way to their final solution, to be made, remade to shade the light is how he put it, and all was quiet, the little boy sat on a pile of newspapers, still half-naked, listening to voices behind the walls while sucking pieces of sugar cubes he had found in a box behind the newspapers, eyes burning with colorful circles he sat there for hours, waiting I suppose for night to fall so he could come out of his hole, his hands groping in the dark, butterflies in the stomach, dust in his mouth at this point the old man started coughing and coughing uncontrollably and a little blood trickled down at the corner of his mouth, we watched him not knowing what to do, then one of us handed him a towel, the cough stopped, he wiped his mouth, took a deep breath, Damn cough, he said, and then he went on with his story

Later, hours later, in the afternoon, guts squeaking with pain, yes the poor kid had to go to the bathroom, and he felt guilty about that, about not being able to do it in the proper place, he unfolded one of the newspapers with pictures of victorious soldiers marching into the city, and crouching like an animal, like a sphinx, he defecated his fear holding his penis away from his legs not to wet himself, then he wrapped it into a neat package, smelling the warmth on his hands afterward, by reflex, and when finally it was dark outside, and the trains were rolling into the night to the east, he climbed the ladder near the door of his closet up to the skylight and placed his filthy package on the roof

the old man looked at us and smiled, for the birds, I suppose, or to disintegrate in the wind and become, years later, the symbol of his strange rebirth, then the boy stepped down the stairs, slowly, one by one, feeling his way in the dark with his hand along the walls, counting each step as if playing a game, but he stumbled on the twelfth step and fell, a door opened and a man shouted, Who's there, he had put on one of his father's overcoats which reached to his ankles, and a dusty fedora which drooped over his eyes, and when he emerged into the courtyard he started running, barefoot, he hadn't found any shoes in the closet, running clumsily toward the hollow of his fate, condemned for the rest of his life to question relentlessly this obscure beginning and never comprehend how that day he had ceased to be a son and became his own father, the old man stopped, raised his hand to his mouth in a gesture of dissatisfaction, I don't like the last part of this story, he said, I'll have to work on it

I have never understood why he told us this story, Moinous says as he reaches for the pack of cigarettes on my desk, you mind, especially that day, and why he kept telling this story over and over again, he even tried to write it once

that's right, Namredef confirms, he showed it to us, the way it was written it was almost unreadable, he had devised a form for it, an unusual typography, perfect squares of words on the pages with no punctuation, no interruptions, it was like a long delirious verbal disarticulation without beginning or end, just boxes of black words prisoner of their own form, he called it The Voice in the Closet, an obscure and disturbing piece of writing, he worked on it for years, used to refer to it as My Season in Hell, an edifice of unreadability in which voices speak within voices in a strange reversal of roles, the voice of fiction accusing the author of having messed up the story, of having failed to tell the real story, from the reverse of farness, as it is said in the text

do you think it's autobiographical, I ask, but both Namredef and Moinous seem tentative

I suppose a man's biography is always something one invents afterwards, after the facts, Namredef replies

usually from beyond the grave, outre-tombe, Moinous amplifies, for the truth of this world is death, one must choose, to die or to lie

how right you are, Namredef says, and fiction is merely the reshaping of old truths into lies, or vice versa

look you guys, this discussion is not getting us anywhere, can we move on

are you familiar with this story, I mean The Voice in the Closet, Namredef asks me

yes I read it once, a long time ago, it's a most puzzling piece of writing, totally incoherent and yet quite moving, I don't think it has ever been properly understood, but that's not the point right now, why don't you guys go on with your report

you mean what happened after he told us the story of the little boy in the closet, oh we just sat on the balcony of the Pensione, the sun was setting, it was a beautiful evening, you know a typical Mediterranean sunset, somehow the telling of that story seemed to have revitalized him and he felt better, Much better, he said, a little color appeared on his face, he stood up stretching his tall slim body, he was bare chested and the ribs showed through his pale skin, he had lost a lot of weight, he leaned on the railing of the balcony, overlooking the sea, Sometimes it amazes me, he said quietly, how I have managed to become a character in my own stories, and how that boy has become a character in my own life, and suddenly he started to laugh, to laugh while coughing, but vigorously, almost hysterically, as if something had snapped inside him

I feel better, so much better, and he went on laughing for days, yes for days, even alone at night standing on the balcony of the Pensione, facing the nubilous sea, we could hear him from our room on the floor below, his room was just above ours, yes we could hear him laughing and laughing fiendishly, as if defying nature and the state of his own illness, and sometimes even talking aloud while laughing, one night he was talking so loud we thought someone was up there with him, though there were no other guests in that Pensione, we got up and quietly walked up the stairs to watch him through the open French windows without him seeing us huddled in the dark, he was bent over the railing as though speaking to someone below, but there was no one there of course

This fucking world is saturated with false hopes, he was screaming, we are drowning in a cesspool of theosophical emanations, cosmic influences, occult powers, spiritual visitations, stellar vibrations and divine farts, and yes yes it's all shit, de la merde molle et fumante, do you hear me, de la saloperie, de la crasse

we let him go on without interfering and went back to our

room, but night after night he stood there laughing and ranting like a lunatic, we thought he was going crazy, and yet quite miraculously, that's the only way one can think of it now, less than two weeks later he was cured, it was amazing, he had simply laughed himself back to health

è stupefacente, è fantastico, the old Sicilian doctor who was taking care of him said after examining him, the spots on his lungs were fading away, disappearing, and the blood no longer came rushing to his throat, he was eating again with his usual gargantuesque appetite, huge plates of pasta, for breakfast, lunch, dinner, ah did he love pasta, did you know that he once wrote a whole novel while living on noodles for a full year, no I'm serious, he called it A Time for Noodles, though later I think he changed the title of that book

anyway he was quickly getting back in shape and one morning he woke us up early and proposed that we all go gambling in Monte Carlo, for a few days, a week, what the hell, he was obsessed by Monte Carlo where in the past he had lost a lot of money, and certainly would lose much more in the future, but he was convinced that some day he would win, Yes one of these days dammit I've got to get lucky and hit it big

he even invited the old doctor to come along, Dire mio caro Dottore, he knew a few words of Italian which he always misused, have you ever been to Monte Carlo, it's the most beautiful place in the world, molto grandioso, si, molto decadent too, but the old Sicilian just shook his head in dismay while mumbling to himself, Dio mio, Dio cane

yes, that's how our old man was, so unpredictable, so changeable, and so careless with his own life, despondent one day, hopeful the next, always more interested in the process than finalities, but then you know him, Moinous says to me, not an easy man to deal with

that afternoon the three of us left Palermo, by ferry to the mainland, and then by train from the bottom of the boot, no of course we didn't have much money, barely enough to keep going, but we didn't give a damn in those days, we borrowed from other people, from friends, from loan sharks, pawned our possessions when the situation was getting desperate, even our typewriters, our scriptodictos when typewriters became outmoded, our watches, our winter clothes as soon as spring arrived, what a life, but the old man always managed to shrug it off with one of his typical statements, I remember just as we were getting off the train in the Monaco station he said, Oui la vie c'est ça, un jour on est prêt à crever et le lendemain bah on dit merde à la vie, always reverting to his native tongue as soon as he stepped on French soil, as if he suddenly felt liberated

we spent a frenzied week of debauchery in Monte Carlo, gambling all night, sleeping or screwing all day, well at least the old guy did, he was mad then, ferocious in his sexual indulgence, as though he wanted to make up the lost time all at once

I don't know if we should tell you this, Namredef hesitates, but one afternoon he took three filles de joie with him up to his room, it was so embarrassing for us, the two friends recall, we were staying in a rather luxurious but stuffy place, he was so sure we were going to win at the casino that he picked the most expensive hotel, but that day, I mean the day he went up to his room with the three whores we were kicked out of that fancy hotel when he was caught chasing one of the girls down the grand circular stairway, he finally grabbed her in the lobby, a short plump giggly brunette with enormous boobs, they were both completely nude, Come here you salope, he shouted, right there in the middle of all the elegant people who stood around in that richly decorated lobby like a display of mannequins, and he carried her up to his room slung over his shoulders, the cheeks of her buttocks shimmering in the light of the crystal chandelier, threw her on the bed flat on her stomach and climbed on top of her, squeezing her nervous body between his hairy legs

you understand, Namredef explains apologetically, we were

not present to witness this scene, it was reported to us years later, more or less as it happened, though undoubtedly some details were omitted

but meanwhile, Moinous goes on, next to them on the bed the other two girls were going at it, embracing, sucking, fingering each other's cunts with wild abandon, Get your ass up, the old man shouted to the brunette between his legs while he shoved a pillow under her stomach, she was still giggling and wiggling, eh arrête de bouger comme ça et lève ton cul cocotte, and when she did he held her by the hips, lifted her into an arch, a bridge of voluptuous flesh, and pushed his cock in full erection into her juicy twat from behind, she moaned happily

I was screwing away, groaning with pleasure, these are his own words, when I felt something tickling my ass, it was wet and discreet, one of the other girls had introduced her tongue in my asshole and was licking it subtly and searchingly while her hands were toying with my balls from around my waist, it was maddening, vas-y mollo mignonne, I told her almost out of control, the third girl meanwhile had moved in front of my face her thighs wide open, offering her furry crotch to my mouth, I lunged forward and plunged my face in it, the four of us formed a complex ensemble of human flesh and sweat, quite a tableau, I tell you even Hans Bellmer couldn't possibly have improved on us, we would certainly have won first prize for best composition à la Biennale de Venise, and we kept on licking, fondling, puffing, fucking, You're driving me nuts I was shouting as I humped away, twisting my body frantically, the girl in front of my face reached for a pack of cigarettes on the nightstand, Gitanes, I still remember, lit one, placed it between her toes and presented it to me, I took a drag, inhaled deeply and let the smoke out slowly as I ejaculated inside the plump brunette, wow did I come, did I unload, and then the four of us collapsed on the bed, arms, legs, tits, asses all unwound, a mess of sweaty giggly flesh

that's when we entered the room, Namredef and Moinous explain to me, together with le directeur de l'hôtel who was screaming and gesticulating angrily, Ah ah vous voyez Messieurs, non vraiment je regrette beaucoup mais vous comprenez ce genre de conduite, dans un établissement comme le nôtre, et en plein jour par-dessus le marché, ah ça alors non, non, we didn't argue, we simply moved to another hotel

I see, how long did he go on like this, I ask, but Namredef and Moinous ignore my question and quickly change the subject

the two of us were losing at the casino, eventually everything we had with us, which was not so much, but the old man had a fabulous streak of luck, one night he hit seven full numbers in a row at the roulette table, imagine seven full numbers at 36 to 1, no 35 to 1, that's what they pay there, but even so, he kept playing the same two numbers each time, the four and the twenty-two, whether or not these two numbers had symbolic meaning for him we don't know, though he did explain to us later that according to the Kabbalah he was a four twenty-two, whatever that means, as you must no doubt be aware the two of us have never been too good with numerology, but in any event that's why he kept playing those two numbers, because he was a four twenty-two, and he won something like a quarter of a million francs that night, honest, oh yes new francs of course, and though Nam and I were broke it didn't matter at all because among ourselves we always shared everything, the spiritual as well as the material, joy as well as sorrow, we formed a perfect trio, yes a perfect triangular association, each complementing the other, each making up for what the other was lacking, especially in character

no doubt about that, I say to myself glancing askance at my two narrators, indeed Moinous so candid and restless, and Namredef always sedate and thoughtful, as for the old geezer a web of complexities and irrationalities, what a delightful combination

with some of that money we bought an Alfa Romeo, a real beauty, brand new, blue convertible with white leather seats, electric windows, wire wheels, Michelin tires, five speeds,

Moinous specifies, he's always the one who pays attention to the little details, and drove two days and two nights straight to Hamburg just to see a performance of Richard Wagner's Parsifal, our old friend had a passion, an irrational passion for that opera, somewhat of a contradiction in terms of his usual taste in other forms of art, and even in terms of his own artistic tendencies which leaned, as you know, toward the esoteric and the ultraprogressive

he insisted on doing all the driving, through the Swiss Alps, the Black Forest, then on to Freiburg, Stuttgart, Frankfurt, Cologne, avoiding the major highways, the busy Autobahns, and without ever consulting the road map we had bought before leaving Monte Carlo, finding his way by intuition and the good fortune of signs on the road, Ici on avance au pifomètre, he smiled pointing to his nose, going north, Hamburg is north, isn't it, and that's where we're going, north, he kept answering when we questioned his sense of direction, but at times we had a feeling he was driving in circles, and on top of that it rained the entire trip, This fucking country is like a pisspot, he kept saying

Nam and I took turns sitting in the narrow uncomfortable back seat where it was impossible even to stretch our legs, this is crazy, totally mad, the two of us kept mumbling, just to see a lousy opera

will you two guys stop bitching, he told us as he pushed on, you have no sense of history

history my ass, what the hell does Wagner's Parsifal have to do with history, this is preposterous, just to see an opera, and what kind of opera, I asked him as we drove through Koblenz, wasn't it Nietzsche who said of Parsifal, on the occasion of its première, I believe, in Bayreuth, Oh what decadence, what a tortured unscrupulous piece of cagliostrism

yes it was Nietzsche, Namredef confirmed, but the old man just shrugged his shoulders, nonetheless, let's be fair, don't you agree Moimoi that it was worth it, an incredible performance

yes very much so, I admit, a memorable evening, an historic six
hour performance at the Hamburgische Staatsoper conducted
by Eugen Jochum, if I remember correctly, with Sven Olof
Eliasson as the lead tenor, grandiose and majestic, but exhausting too

the old man was all excited, One really understands the German mind, and especially Nazism, listening to this kind of
music, he said as we walked out of the auditorium into the
brightly lit lobby of the opera house, he was all worked up,
both exhilarated and tense, Watching such a demented spectacle makes one understand why Nazism and Fascism are considered obscene and pornographic forms of modern revival, yes
desperate revivals of Machiavellian political power, the violent
reactivation of a power that despairs of its own rational basis

whenever our old man got started like this the best thing to do
was to let him go on until he ran out of steam, but we did say to
him, Can you control youself a bit, keep your voice down, we
were surrounded by all these Germans who were pouring out
of the auditorium, most of them silent and mechanical in their
gestures, as though still crushed by the performance they had
just witnessed

he ignored us, Wagner with his naive neoromantic agony pre-
pared the way for Nazism, knowing full well what he was
doing, his mysticopolitical masquerades are forerunners of Hitler's hysterical Hollywoodian spectacles, ah Hitler, the greatest
of all metteurs en scène ever

we were still in the lobby of the opera house and we had a
feeling people around us were trying to listen to what the old
man was saying, but he went on, almost arrogant in his attitude

You know, Nazism is fascinating, and frightening too of
course, because it defies all political truths and assumes its
power until death, its own as well as that of others, it is
cunningly phantasmagorial and tragically self-destructive, it
learned to replay the ritualistic prestige of death, by overbid-
ding, by overstaging, but in a manner that is totally fake and

already posthumous at its birth, and as such no longer sacrificial, no longer cathartic, Nazism's politics is death, a politics of extinction performed under the pretense of unlimited etatism and the oneiric exhaltation of a superior blood which implies the systematic extermination of others while rejoicing in total self-annihilation

dammit, will you shut up, and let's get out of here, we said to him while pulling him by the sleeves of his coat

No I will not, let me speak, and he went on, louder even, you see my dear friends, Nazism is based on a retroactive aesthetic, and whatever is retroactive can inspire itself only of an obscenity and a violence already nostalgic when it happens, Nazism, Fascism, and of course this is true of all the other isms, including Communism, are retrogressive scenarios of power and of death already obsolete, already played out at the very moment when they appear in history, and that too is the meaning of Parsifal, a clever displacement of the Second Coming, or as Kafka once pointed out, a false announcement of the possible apparition of the Messiah, and I suppose that's what Nietzsche meant by decadence and unscrupulousness, yes an eternal simulation of a dying internal power that can only be the sign of what has been, what has died, so you see that's why Parsifal is such a fraudulent historic retroversion

so why do you like this opera so much, we asked him, why did you drive us crazy to come and see this thing

I like it as a work of art, it's a gutsy work of art, the old man replied, and I like Wagner's music even though I hate the false ideology it peddles, its pretentiousness

Isn't that contradictory, we remarked

Everything in art is contradictory, don't you know that

he kept staring at the Germans as he spoke, staring at them without any self-consciousness, all of them elegantly dressed, stern, quiet, as though subdued, seduced by the six hour performance they had just watched, and who wouldn't be, all of them looking dangerously rich and complacent, it was raining outside so most of them were still gathered in the lobby of the opera house

Let's get the fuck out of here, the old man suddenly said as he rushed us into the street

I don't understand why you get so worked up, Namredef told his old friend, I really don't get it, after all you're the one who wanted to come here, who drove forty-eight hours like a maniac to get us here, the old man was walking in long strides, almost running, Namredef and Moinous trotting along to keep up with him, they are both short and a bit flabby, Is it because you're Jewish, asked Namredef totally out of breath, I'm Jewish too and I don't get excited like you when I am in the midst of Germans, you can't blame them all, is it because your entire family was exterminated by the Nazis, so what, mine too was remade into lampshades at Auschwitz, or have you forgotten

And mine too, mine too, intervened Moinous who was holding on to his side as he trotted along splashing in the rain

the old man shrugged his shoulders, It has nothing to do with that, and besides I'm not worked up, I'm just being philosophical, that's all, the two of you always confuse ideology with sentiment, yes it's amazing how you two schnorrers always have to reduce everything to your Jewish sentimentality

oh you people didn't know Namredef and Moinous are Jewish too, well I haven't mentioned it because I thought it was obvious, and anyway this is not their story, they are incidental here, they have been introduced simply for the convenience of the narrative, to help along, to allow some shifts of point of view and some creative free play

we dropped the subject, the old man was getting angry, but later, as we sat in the enclosed terrace of the Kaffeehaus Bis-

marck, facing the Aussenalster, enjoying Kaffee mit Schlag-
sahne and a slice of Haselnusstorte, our old man was quite a
gourmand, we went on with the discussion

Personally I don't see what relationship there is between Wagner's Parsifal and the Jewish problem, Moinous said as if he had
totally missed the point of the discussion, no quite frankly I
don't see what it has to do with the question of Jewish sentimentality

Who said there is a relationship, the old man shouted, and
anyway I didn't bring up the subject, you guys did

Okay, but why did you get so upset before, Namredef asked,
don't tell me it wasn't because of that performance

I was not upset, I was just reflecting, that's all, but since you
guys are that concerned let me tell you something about the
Jewish question, it is never a matter of sentiment, but a matter
of political strategy, the oppression of Jews always begins as a
game and ends as a crime, it always turns out badly because it
confuses two obscure realities, on the one side the questioned
Jew threatened in his singularity, on the other the questioner,
the anti-semite who presents himself as the spokesman of a
generality, of a totality, the people, the community, the nation,
the race, but these two realities are in fact undefinable, for what
is Jewish singularity, is it an attitude, a memory, an event, a
nose or a circumcised cock, a series of rituals, is it languages or
echoes of languages, yes it is indeed difficult to grasp by what
sneaky operation all this can be transposed into a syrupy and
homogenous universality, or what is called a Jewish identity,
because you see Jews are not different from others, as racism
would have us believe, what Jews show us with their undying
presence is the relation of difference which the human face
brings into revelation and entrusts to our responsibility, and
even Wagner knew that

Oh that's well said, Moinous interjected

And that is why, the old man continued, we were back at the

hotel in Hamburg, sitting in his room, he was all excited again, he got up and started pacing, banging his fist on the furniture as he went back and forth, good solid German furniture, Yes that's why to exclude the Jews, no, really, that does not suffice, to exterminate them, that is not enough, they would have to be erased from history, removed from the books in which they have spoken to humanity, their presence would have to be obliterated once and for all, before and after all books, their stubborn presence which is inscribed words through which man, as far back as one can remember, already turned toward man, in other words, to get rid of the Jews one would have to suppress all the others, and that is what that halfassed corporal Hitler never understood, you can destroy flesh, you can make lampshades out of dried skin, but you cannot destroy words, they survive in the corridors of history, and since Jews and books have always been synonymous, Jabès taught us that, then Judaism and writing are but the same expectation, the same hope, the same erosion

You're damn right, Namredef and Moinous said in unison, like one man, heads shaking in approval, as the old man disappeared into the bathroom, I'm going to take a quick shower, he yelled from behind the door, I'll be out in a few minutes

we stood silently by the window looking out at the city, pondering what the old man had just said, a thick fog was descending over the city, and suddenly we heard the siren of a distant tug boat whine into the night, it was quite late

when the old man came out of the bathroom he was all dressed, overcoat and all

Where are you going, we asked

Okay you two, get off your ass and let's go win some money, Where, where at this time of night, Moinous asked, In Lübeck, he was rubbing his hands together, What, Lübeck, Moinous looked puzzled, at this late hour, Oh sure, there is a casino there, a fancy one too I understand, stays open all the time, and it's only an hour or so from here

Hey that's a terrific idea, Moinous said with a childish glimmer in his eyes, this way we can see Thomas Mann's house, I always wanted to visit the old Buddenbrook, it's in Lübeck, isn't it

Holy cow Moinous, the old man sneered, you mean to say you go for that kind of touristic crap

Well, it's a good occasion, no, Moinous insisted, and besides who knows when we'll have another chance

Come on Moimoi, don't tell me you give a shit about ruins, especially reconstructed ruins, gambling that's why we're going there, old buddy, and not to visit some miserable relics of a decadent society, forget about Thomas Mann's house, gambling, yes at the Travemünde Casino, that's where we're going, so grab your coats and let's go, I feel lucky

that old guy is really something else, and so off we went into the night, full speed on the Autobahn in our little Alfa Romeo, but an hour later, as we drove past Thomas Mann's house in the center of Lübeck, our old guy, to our surprise, started reciting the last lines of Buddenbrooks which he said he once learned by heart, when I was in college, wow that's a long time ago, just for the fun of it, I liked the sound of the words, and the way the syntax moves, She stood there, a victor in the good fight which all her life she had waged against the assaults of reason, humpbacked, tiny, quivering with the strength of her convictions, a little prophetess, admonishing and inspired

you know, the old man paused, I think when Thomas Mann wrote these lines he was not only describing a disillusioned woman, Fräulein Sesemi Weichbrodt, I believe that's her name, but the house itself, Buddenbrook, that monument of pride and complacency, and beyond that the city itself, Lübeck, yes Lübeck that old city of many lives and many deaths, city of connivance, of sickness and genius, of decadence and culture, city where the corrosion of the will to survive goes hand in hand with a spirituality that accepts death passively, and you know something, that's what Germany is all about, a

double-headed monster of duplicity, Thomas Mann understood that, and he made of this duplicity his aesthetic and
philosophical principle, that's why the Nazis expelled him,
they could not accept the truth, but he knew, and he was so
right when he wrote that the mind here is hatred that plays, and
art a nostalgia that creates, both live in a country of dupes, of
starved people, of accusers and negators, yes Thomas Mann
understood that the German penchant for philosophical ideal-
ism is a mask for social hypocrisy and brutalization

I don't know what prompted this morbid reflection in our old
man, Namredef says as he interrupts his narrative, he did not
elaborate, certainly not the sight of that rather impressive
house, no, I suppose he was still reacting to Wagner's opera, or
something more personal, but imagine that, here we were,
driving through Lübeck in the middle of the night, and he was
lecturing to us

anyway we drove on to the casino, just across the Trave River,
we didn't play, Namredef and Moinous explain, we only
watched, the old man stood close to the roulette wheel and
stared at the little white ball as though trying to hypnotize it,
and when it kept rolling into the four and into the twenty-two,
again and again, he was stubbornly faithful to his lucky numbers, he barely flinched, barely showed any emotion, he simply
gathered his chips, casually, arrogantly, tossing large pieces
toward the croupiers, Pour les employés, he would say with
disdain, Vielen Dank mein Herr, pour les employés who
looked at him in awe as if he were some godlike figure even
though that night he looked rather beat, rather shabby, and not
at all like a Gottesmensch

he had not shaved in four days, and the sexual orgies of Monte
Carlo, the long exhausting drive to Hamburg, the Wagnerian
musical marathon had left their mark on his face, in his eyes
especially

Oui, il avait plutôt une sale gueule, Moinous says, not finding
the right words in English to describe the piteous physical

condition of his friend, he looked haggard, but that did not affect his luck, nor his arrogance, non pas du tout, he was incredible that night

Namredef and Moinous could not remember how much he won, but it was an amazing sum of money, he collected it all in small bills, he insisted on that, thousands of them in small denominations, just to have the impression of having won even more than he did, he made the cashier shove the money into bags, you know those large plastic bags, greenish garbage bags, eight of them, I remember, and at dawn we drove back to Hamburg, in a dense fog, he was driving, madly, furiously, almost out of control, the road was hardly visible, He's going to get us killed, we kept saying to each other, but he ignored us, he didn't speak during the entire trip, except once, once to himself, when he said in a murmur, Never again, Never again

back in his hotel room he looked at us with a strange smile on his face and then told us, quite unexpectedly, It is said that in the bunker where Hitler and his cohorts were spending their last night, making their last stand, the generals and field marshals who still had illusions of grandeur masturbated Hitler and made him ejaculate into a little vial, and that one of them, Feldmarschall von Schleischer, left the bunker under cover of darkness and went to a prearranged location in Switzerland where he buried the little vial in a secret place so that one day when the perfect Aryan woman is found she can be artificially inseminated for the resurrection and give birth to Hitler the Second

You're making this up, we cried outraged, what a disgusting story, it's so ridiculous

Look, you guys can believe whatever you want, but it's true, he said as he began to undress, it's true, wait and see, he was naked now, then he spread the bills on the floor, bundles of them, those large Deutschmark, made a bed of them, a nest, and lay on top, still naked, rolled in them, crawled in them like a giant worm, tossing the bills into the air and letting them fall on his body, rubbing them against his chest, his stomach, his penis, he even shoved some in his mouth while laughing hysterically

we left him, there was something painful in watching this pale body twist in the paper money

The order of the world conceals intolerable disorders, I say to my two narrators as they go on with their report

late that afternoon when we came back to wake him we found him buried under the crumpled bills, some of them stained with sweat and sperm, and shit, he had jerked off wildly in the Deutschmark, masturbated and crapped in that money like an animal, like a little boy enraged by the pain of unfulfilled desire, and as we stood there we heard him laugh again, yes laugh and giggle in his sleep as he tossed, we watched him for a few moments, embarrassed at first, somewhat horrified, and then we too started laughing, like two clowns, what else could we do, yes like two dejected clowns who have messed up their act, but since he would not wake up, we left again and went for a stroll on the Reeperbahn

Do you think he's going crazy, Namredef asked Moinous

No, I think he is simply readjusting to the idea that he is still alive, I agree he has a strange way of doing it, but it's understandable, you know he was very close to death, I don't think you and I fully realized in Palermo how sick he was, we thought the old Sicilian doctor was exaggerating, dramatizing his illness like any typical Latin, but it was serious, believe me, and now he is reinserting himself into life with mad laughter

It's not that unusual, I interrupt Moinous, those who have stared death in the eyes, as the saying goes, often come back in a state of hilarity, it's been proven, because you see laughter is essentially a philosophical act, in fact that's exactly what his old Rumanian friend Cioran once wrote him in a letter, yes I remember, he showed it to me, and as you know survival is a kind of philosophy of life

Yes we know, Namredef butts in somewhat annoyed by my interruption, many people spend their entire lives surviving, but did he have to do it with such madness, I mean with such vehemence, such vengeance

Perhaps not, Moinous says, but the capacity of man for life is certainly a form of madness, don't you think so, we accept the idea of death but not the time of our own death, to die any time, eventually, later, that's okay, yes that's acceptable, in principle, nothing we can do about that, but when it is time to die, when the ultimate moment is here, no, that we cannot accept, we panic, whine, drop all our self-respect, only a few are able to laugh in the face of death, I myself have experienced such madness, such hilarious madness, Moinous says his voice suddenly becoming melodramatic, I was stabbed in the chest some years ago, in another version of my life you might say, right next to the heart, yes right here, Moinous clutches his breastbone, it happened in a bar in San Francisco, The Blue Bird, ah do I remember that dive

the old man was supposed to meet me there, he was driving across country but he was late, delayed, got stranded in a snowstorm one night in his old beat-up Buickspecial, a 1947 I think it was, the damn car jumped over an embankment into a precipice but luckily it landed on top of a tree, a pine tree, no I'm not exaggerating, a Christmas tree covered with snow, that's how he described it, quite a trick, the car got stuck in the branches and when he managed to work his way out of the wreck, that General Motors pile of junk, as he called it, body by Fisher, he found himself suspended there like an angel, asking himself what the hell he was doing up there hanging from a branch like a Christmas ornament, Jesus Christ, he cried into the night, what a ridiculous situation, but eventually he was rescued by some gorgeous woman, a stunning blonde who happened to be driving by and saw him stretched out in the snow, it's quite a story, you should have heard him tell it, and of course that old pervert made it with the blonde and that's the reason he was delayed

the two of us were leaving for the Far East on the same boat, we were in the army at the time, the U.S. Army, and were being shipped to Korea, Namredef had already left on another boat, isn't that right Nam, that was one of the few times we were separated, Nam and I, but of course I never made it overseas, I was stabbed in the chest, the old man however was reunited with Namredef in a foxhole near Inchon after all sorts of misadventures, but that's another story

meanwhile everybody in that San Francisco bar thought I was dead, finished, I was taken to the morgue, but when the coroner was tying the orange identification tag of the moribund on my big toe he tickled me and I reacted, you guys are laughing but it's true, I moved, oh not much, just a touch, but that's when the coroner realized I wasn't dead, you should have seen his face, he was astonished, he almost fainted, imagine that, it was as though I were resurrected, up from the dead, they rushed me to a hospital, I was laughing, the knife had missed the heart by that much, I mean that much, Moinous brings his thumb and index finger together allowing just a little space between them, a silly millimeter, he says tittering at the cleverness of his own analogy, I couldn't stop laughing for days afterward, even in the hospital, ask the old man, he came to visit me every day when he found out where I was, even brought me some choco-lates, that was nice of him, I couldn't control myself, it was like I had permanent giggly contractions of the diaphragm, it just came bursting out of me, mad hilarity, and it was contagious, the whole place became a laughing madhouse, everybody caught it, the doctors, the interns, nurses, cleaning women, all the other patients, the visitors, everybody was laughing with me, philosophically you might say

they caught the person who stabbed me by the way, he was just a kid, not even sixteen years old, sort of blondish and freckled, I can still see his face, with a sweet mouth, what the hell he was doing in that bar I'll never know, they brought him to my room in the hospital and I asked him between two guffaws, Why did you do it, and do you know what he answered, that lousy kid, I don't know Sir, I really don't know, I couldn't stop myself, maybe it was because of the way you were looking at me Sir or something, goddammit I don't even remember looking at the bastard, didn't even notice him in that crowded bar, I was minding my own business, I was on my second or maybe my third beer, wondering where the hell the old guy was when, swissh, right in the chest, just like that

Yes we know that story, I say to Moinous, it's been told before, by the old man in Tioli, we all stood over your dead body, in Tioli, Moinous looks vexed, Okay I was just trying to make a point

I understand, but this is not the place, this is not your story, but then Namredef also starts telling us how he too nearly escaped death when he was a paratrooper and made a combat jump in Korea, a night jump, and his chute failed to open and all he could do was laugh, laugh like an idiot, I quickly interrupt him before things get out of hand, Hey you two guys are really something else, don't you think you're going too far, can't you see you're interfering with the progress of this story, we're not interested in your personal affairs, true or false, we are interested in the old man's life, past and future, and his present predicament, have you forgotten, I don't think it's necessary to remind you of the urgency of this situation, all that stuff about immortality is a weak alibi, don't you think you should get back to him before it's too late, before he disappears, rather than waste more time with your anecdotes, maybe some other time we'll give you a chance to tell your sordid tales

they both agree, even though somewhat disheartened, and continue their report

hours later when we returned to his room in that hotel in Hamburg to try and wake him again, he was gone, his clothes were piled up on the floor, he must have emptied his suitcase to put the money in it, on the table we found a stack of Deutschmark, for us we presumed, how thoughtful of him, also the keys of the Alfa Romeo, and two words scribbled in red, almost illegibly, on a piece of toilet paper, Moinous thought it said, Temporarily Saved, but Namredef argued that it really said, Temporarily Sane, that was all, he had left, just like that, and in a way we were not surprised

===== VI =====

Several months passed before we found him again

what had happened to him, I inquired when Namredef and
Moinous returned from one of their investigations

he had settled in Paris for a while, sort of trying to put himself
back together, we found him by chance, ran into him one night
in a café, at two in the morning, Avenue du Maine in Montparnasse, one of those typical proletarian cafés, he was playing
billiards with two pimps, yes two tough-looking Parisian
maqueraux, do you remember Moinous

yes, two rather mean-looking characters, deux malabars à la
branque avec des gueules de corsaires, and were they drunk, I
mean the two pimps, it was strange seeing him in such company

what were you two guys doing there at that time

oh nothing, nothing much, just bumming around, going on as
best we could, feeling sort of useless, hoping, hoping that
perhaps, but you know, without him we were nothing

he didn't notice us at first when we walked into that café for a late cognac, no I don't think he saw us, or else pretended not to see us, he went on playing billiards, three cushion, congratulating the two pimps for the great shots they were making, ça alors vous les mecs vous êtes vachement forts hein, though I must say he was damn good himself, making incredible shots, series of fifteen or twenty points at a time, obviously hustling the two pimps

we watched the game from our table, keeping track of the score mentally, he was a fine billiard-player, I don't think we've mentioned it before, his father had taught him how to play when he was a little boy, he was a quick learner, he even won several championships, international championships, in fact his name is still listed in L'Encyclopédie Mondiale du Billard, you can look it up if you wish, page 394 in the 37th edition published by La Maison Stock, he perfected le triple coup retro à effet anglais, better known as le coup bancal, but now he will never again be able to indulge in his favorite pastime once he reaches the colonies, no he won't, they must have abolished billiards out there

he looked terrible, pale and dirty, he had grown a beard, a long shaggy beard which made him look older than he was then, and somewhat repellent, he was wearing a worn-out pair of brown corduroy pants and a torn black turtleneck sweater, Moinous gave that information, as usual picking out the little details

Ah ça merde alors, if it isn't Nam and Moimoi, what are you doing here, he shouted from across the room leaning dissolutely on his cue when he finally saw us, or when he finally decided to acknowledge our presence, Where have you been, just like that, as though we were the ones who had left him in Hamburg, who had split without any warning or reason, yes as though we were the ones who somehow should feel guilty about leaving him, Haven't seen you two bums for months, he said, just like that, with casual effrontery as he came toward us, Yes must be a good seven or eight months, I was worried about you, kept wondering where the hell you'd disappeared to, he embraced us with real affection, we didn't know what to say, we didn't try to argue, no we didn't even question him about his sudden disappearance, we were so glad to have found him again

Would you like a drink or something, we asked, a cognac

Hé dis machin tu joues ou tu joues plus, the two pimps yelled from the billiard table obviously annoyed by this disturbance and this show of emotion, t'as pas fini de nous faire poireauter

Ah allez-vous faire voir, je joue plus, he shouted back as he threw his cue across the room like a spear almost hitting one of the pimps in the face, and immediately the two brutes rushed toward us, one of them with a knife in his hand, a switchblade which he had slipped out of his sleeve, imagine that, the sneaky sonofabitch

Hé calmez-vous les gars, faut pas s'exciter comme ça quoi, c'est deux vieux copains que je viens de retrouver par hasard, said the old man as he stood in front of us protecting us with his body, arms outstretched in front of him as if holding back an oncoming cavalry charge with invisible power, the two pimps hesitated, stopped, wow they looked mean, vraiment vaches, but the old guy meant business, it was clear, Un pas de plus et je vous démolis, je vous ratatine sur place, he said as he grabbed a chair and held it above his head, just like in a cowboy movie, all we needed at this point was a little bugle call

Moinous and I meanwhile were already out of the door observing the scene from the sidewalk, totally helpless, the three or four other drunks in the café had also cleared out, the old man backed off slowly toward the exit while le patron du café, an obese bovine of a man wrapped in a blue tablier, was screaming, Arrêtez bande de cons ou j'appelle les poulets, but the pimp with the knife took the blade with two fingers and threw it at the old man, who the fuck did he think he was, Pépé le Moko, the blade skimmed the old man's arm just above the elbow, the left one, and blood spurted out, Espèce de salopard, enculé, and as he said that the old man hit the pimp on the head with the chair, and I mean hard with all his strength, but unlike those fake chairs in Hollywood movies this one did not break into pieces, the pimp fell to the floor like a sack of sawdust, unconscious, while the other pimp retreated to the back of the café, the old man hurled the chair across the room, Pourri, enfoiré, he shouted again as he ran into the street full speed down Avenue du Maine where one could already hear the Pin-Pon of the police cars, we followed him, turned on the double into Rue de la Gaieté until we were sure we had lost the two pimps

Hey that was close, the old man said smiling as he wrapped his arms around our shoulders, you guys look like you're scared shitless, and indeed Moinous and I were trembling and puffing like two water buffaloes, not that we are cowards, but the whole thing had happened so quickly

Hey thanks, you were tremendous, we told him, you really flattened that puny proxénète, I tell you, you were terrific

Yeah, but did you see those two motherfuckers, who the hell do they think they are, he was rubbing his hands together with vigorous satisfaction, we had never known him to be that violent, on the contrary, more like him to talk or double-talk his way out of a fight, in French, in English, or even in both simultaneously, no he was not the sort of guy who goes around punching people in the mouth

but he was obviously pleased with himself, standing there, Rue de la Gaieté, still rubbing his hands

How is your arm, we asked

It's okay, it's nothing, just a scratch, but dammit did I knock the shit out of that pimp, did you see that

Maybe you should see a doctor, we suggested

Come on you guys leave me alone, it's nothing I said, and he brushed us aside, let's go we started walking toward Boulevard du Montparnasse when he suddenly stopped in the middle of Rue Delambre and said, These French pithecanthropes are the last survivors of a slow cataclysm, they live out the death of our planet as the gods of the theogony lived through its ridiculous birth, they are as monstrously comic as these dumb gods were, he shook his head, they typify the last form of homo sapiens as cosmopithecoids

nothing much we could say to that, but then he added with a note of sadness in his voice, Seriously my friends, sometimes I'm ashamed to be part of the same race, ashamed to speak the same language as these idiots, but I suppose one doesn't choose one's mother tongue

we were passing in front of La Coupole, it was still open, How about a drink you guys, come on I'll treat you

we found a table on the terrace which was still packed with people, the artsy types, we ordered three Calvados, and then after a while we asked, But tell us, what have you been doing since you left us in Hamburg, and where did you go, you could have told us you were leaving

Oh I just wanted to be alone, I needed to do some serious thinking, and besides I don't see why you guys are complaining, didn't I leave you some money and the keys to the car

That's not the point, yes we appreciated that, but you could have waited for us, we could have discussed the situation, but instead nothing, you just took off, but okay, where did you go

I went to the Bahnhof and jumped on the first train that came along, it was going to Munich, what the hell, why not Munich, I had never been there, I had stuffed the money we won in Lübeck into my suitcase, there was enough there to last me for quite a while

I found a first class compartment almost empty, only two

persons in it, an American with a young woman, his girl friend, he was a movie director from Hollywood, in fact turns out he is quite well known, has directed all kinds of movies, westerns and war movies, his name is Henry Marcowsky, have you heard of him, yes a Jew, the young woman with him was a starlet, younger than he was by a good twenty years, very striking, blonde, I mean a natural blonde with blue eyes, and legs that go on forever, you know the Grace Kelly type, waspish to her fingertips, and obviously screwing her way into prominence, but with a certain class, she first spoke to me

they didn't know how to make me out, I must have looked terrible, and of course the French accent, but when I told them I too lived in America they became friendly and talkative, they were going to Munich for a few days, sightseeing, but also to visit Dachau, the concentration camp, he wanted to see the place for personal reasons, You understand, he said, I suppose he had guessed I am Jewish, you know the nose, the face, and my name of course, Yes for sentimental reasons

as for the Grace Kelly starlet, she was just tagging along, looking around, her first trip to Germany, After all, she said, everybody feels something about the concentration camps, I feel I should see one of those places at least once in my life, and besides, she had marvelous white teeth, and besides Hank is going to direct a movie that takes place in a concentration camp, that's why he wants to see this camp, for the layout, And for other reasons too, Hank quickly intervened, Grace Kelly went on, I might even have a part in it, wouldn't I be wonderful in that kind of a movie, of course I won't be able to play one of the Jewish women because of my hair and my blue eyes, but you know they were not all Jews in the camps, there were lots of Christians too, Catholics and Protestants

Yes, of course, there were, and Atheists too, I said, I think you'll make a marvelous little martyr

we went on talking as the train rolled along through the German countryside, I asked them about their trip, where they had been, what they had seen, we even discussed some of Hank's movies, they did most of the talking, I was only asking questions to make conversation, but later, as we sat in the dining car for a snack, I said, Hey would you mind if I went with you to Dachau, I think I would like to see it too, might be interesting, and, after all

Of course, Hank replied, we'll be delighted to have you along, a real pleasure, isn't that right Darling, Oh yes, Grace Kelly said with a wet smile, do join us, so it was all set, and besides that blonde starlet had magnificent eyes

we arrived in Munich late that afternoon, since I didn't have a hotel reservation they suggested I try theirs, we took a taxi together to the Königshof on Karlsplatz, quite a luxurious hotel, but hell, I had lots of dough with me in my suitcase, I even went out later, after we checked in, and bought myself a new shirt and tie, a pair of socks, some underwear, a toothbrush and a good German Braun razor, as you know I had left all that behind in Hamburg, and the next morning after a good breakfast we took the train to Dachau

it's just outside of Munich, about forty-five minutes by train, plus a short bus ride from the Dachau station, I was not nervous, nor excited, I don't know what I felt, in fact I really didn't know why I had decided to go, who needs that kind of self-flagellation, sure I had deep personal reasons for wanting to visit a concentration camp, I don't need to tell you that, but what could I see there that was not already in my head, what could I learn

the director was a bit edgy, as for Grace Kelly, she was all bubbly, and sexy in her purple outfit, she had taken her camera with her, and an umbrella, In case it rains, she said, she was wearing a pair of huge sun glasses, we made quite a trio

but soon there were four of us, on the train from Munich to Dachau we met an old lady, sixty or sixty-five years old, Middle-aged, middle-aged, she kept correcting me, an American widow from Teaneck New Jersey, you know, big black eyes, well-set dyed beige hair, the type of woman who walks around with her heart in her hands, she was sitting next to me on the train and so we started talking, You're also going to Dachau, she asked, Yes, we told her, Oh I'm so glad to have met you, I am so nervous about going there alone, you mind if I join you, I won't make a nuisance of myself, and then in a whisper, covering her mouth with one hand she asked me, You're Jewish, aren't you

this was her first trip to Europe, ever, My poor husband passed away last year, may his soul rest in peace, we always promised ourselves to take this trip, now with the little money he left me from the dry cleaning business I finally decided to go, you know, it's a Mitzvah, she explained, she was traveling alone going from one camp to another, she had already been to Buchenwald, and now Dachau, and next she was going to visit Mauthausen, and then Auschwitz, she would love to go to Treblinka, But that's too far, and besides it's almost in Russia, others visit museums and Gothic cathedrals, but she, Miriam was her name, Miriam Millstein, was visiting concentration camps, chacun son goût

Oh no, I was in America during the whole thing, she answered when I asked her if she was a survivor, in fact I was born in the Bronx, but it doesn't matter, you know, because all of us Jews have suffered the same from all that, ah such a tragedy, so you understand why I feel it's a duty, a sacred duty to see these camps

yes indeed Miriam wanted to see, she wanted to splash her sentimentality all over these places, she had to share retrospectively in the collective suffering, and the collective guilt, and why not

we arrived in the town of Dachau, drab and busy, one of those totally reconstructed German towns where all the buildings look like caserns, suddenly we felt this was it, and when the bus stopped in front of the walls and we saw the barbed wire, the tall light posts, the neatly repainted guard towers, we fell silent, and yet somehow I had expected something more terrifying

bus loads of people were arriving, groups of nuns and priests, tourists, school children with their teachers, German children, I heard some Israelis speaking Hebrew next to me, what the hell was I doing here, but it was too late, we were already inside, inside the vast empty space of the camp where the barracks once stood, only two or three buildings remain intact, the rest is only shown on a huge map, a plan which explains how the camp was at one time, where the various barracks stood, what the function of each was, but now they have placed long beams of wood to mark the exact space and dimension of these destroyed barracks, large empty rectangles with pebbles covering the inside surface

we looked for a moment at the intricate piece of sculpture which was erected as a memorial, not bad, social realism with twisted human figures all meshed together and stretching for almost forty feet, we stood in front of it, our starlet took pictures, the movie director was pensive, he kept whirling about as though measuring the space around him, he even scribbled something in a little notebook, Miriam came closer to me, I am sick to my stomach, she said, Oh you'll be all right, I told her, you'll see, if I know the Germans it's presented just right

and indeed it was, nothing offensive, nothing too disturbing here, in fact nothing much to see, except for the huge space where the barracks once were, the map explained everything in detail, where the dining room was, the hospital, the laundry, the showers, the crematorium, that building still stands but we didn't go in, and in the center of the space two memorials, one to the Christians who died here, the other for the Jews

we walked into the main building, the museum, which used to be, a sign explained, the hospital where experiments on human beings were conducted, but aside from this note everything was well presented, correctly, soberly, and intelligently, Those fucking Germans really pulled it off, I said to Marcowsky, a nice mixture of decorum and hygiene, a perfect sense of the tragic but without the horror, just as it should be, and yet

we stood around a while in the large crowded entrance hall before going into the museum proper, I was surprised there was no entrance fee, perhaps at the end there will be a box for donations

on a large table were displays of all sorts of information material in several languages, and souvenirs, one could also buy post-cards, and a book with photographs that recount the history of Dachau, like a catalog, Fifteen Marks, nicely done, Miriam was buying postcards by the dozens, she showed me one she partic-ularly liked, the famous entrance to Dachau with the unforget-table words forged in the gate, Arbeit Macht Frei, she had also bought the catalog, Aren't you buying one of these programs, she asked me, No I don't think so, I really don't want to give them any of my money, Oh let me buy it for you, I insist, I really want to, I suppose it made her feel a little better

I suddenly felt like getting out of there, I had seen enough, but then we walked into the museum, I had moved away from Miriam and I was next to the starlet now, she seemed thought-ful and uneasy, not really sure perhaps that she should be here

let me tell you, my friends, that damn museum is quite some-thing, really nicely done, I mean well presented, well orga-nized, coherent, educational, they have these large panels of photographs and documents that retrace the history of the camp, and other camps too, the rise of Hitler and Nazism, huge enlarged pictures, extremely well presented, chronologically, at first it's like walking into a giant book, or watching a documentary, you see lots of photographs of Hitler and his cohorts, Goering, Goebbels, Himmler, the important mo-ments in Munich, in Berlin, the Reichstag burning, nothing too shocking, you learn that Dachau was established as far back as 1932, no not for the Jews at first, they arrived later, but as a work camp for political prisoners, undesirables, and others too, communists, foreigners, non-aryans, you know, the rabble, the canaille and so you walk through this neatly arranged labyrinth of photographs and documents, you follow the arrows that guide you through Nazi history, you read the captions, the explanations, in your own language, the starlet was not too familiar with all that, so she kept asking me questions and I would go into a little history for her, Oh look, she said suddenly, somebody has erased Hitler's face, and indeed there were many photographs of Hitler where the face had been cut out, scratched out, mutilated with a knife or a sharp object in futile gestures of anger, of rage, or perhaps of revenge on the part of previous visitors, I wondered if those in charge of the museum had to replace these damaged photographs regularly, and if they kept duplicates in stock

Hank was wandering about by himself, doing his thing, Miriam caught up with us, It's quite something eh, much better than Buchenwald, I mean the way it's presented here, it makes more sense, also here they give you a lot more information

I was watching the other people around us, most of them foreigners, but a lot of Germans too, they all had their serious faces on, they moved slowly, quietly, sometimes grabbing the arm of the person with them as they pointed to a stunning and more explicit photograph, one which revealed perhaps more than was originally intended, we were moving too slowly, I wanted to get to the core of this thing, see the real images, those that were inscribed inside my head, all that early historical stuff was merely a show of uniforms and data, but perhaps that's how it should be, a gradual descent into the circles of hell, though as we walked from panel to panel inside this giant picture album, I could feel the tenseness, the emotion rising around me, and then we turned a corner and there before us that huge monstrous photograph of all these dead bodies piled in a communal hole with soldiers walking on top of the bodies, you know which one, it's been shown so many times, the ultimate product of the final solution, Miriam started sobbing aloud, as if she had been holding back for this specific moment, tears were also rolling down Grace Kelly's face, she pulled out a little gold cross on a chain from under the neck of her sweater and kissed it, Hank was next to her, he took her hand and squeezed it, and me, I had a sudden nervous cough, it was the only time I felt sick, sick to my stomach, as Miriam had said earlier

though I did feel the same malaise, the same horror, a few moments later when I came upon another huge photograph which showed a train arriving in Auschwitz and I looked at the faces of the Jews staring back at me, I put my glasses on to see better and try to recognize some of these faces, but the picture had been so enlarged, so stretched out, that the faces were all blurry and unrecognizable

Can you believe this, Miriam kept saying, how horrible, horrible, I felt sorry for her, sorry that she imposed such torment on herself, but I said nothing to her

I was walking with Hank now, talking, You know, I told him, what this reminds me of, I once visited the Ford Company Museum in Dearborn, near Detroit, and it's presented just like this, large panels of photographs and documents which retrace the history of the Ford automobile, from the beginning to the present, you see the factories, the workers on the line, the machines, you see the different models over the years, the Model T, the 1926, the 1932, the 1958, and so on, you see pictures of all the members of the Ford family, all the Henrys, you see the innovations, the improvements, it's really something

we were walking faster now, hardly looking at the pictures or reading the documents, except once, we stopped a long time in front of the photograph of a little boy with big black eyes, he was wearing a French béret and had a yellow star on his coat which was too big for him, he sat on the curb of a street, all alone, with his little bundle tucked next to him, for a moment I thought it was a picture of me

Yes, it's the same principle, I went on explaining to Hank, the same format of presentation, it's the principle of the corporate museum built to show the history of the making of a product, the Ford in this case, a monument to our modern world and man's ingenuity

we had reached the end of the show and found ourselves in a large empty space, along the walls were bookcases with glass doors and inside these a collection of books written about the Holocaust, in many languages, The only difference, I said to Hank who was still listening to me intently, is that at the end of your visit to the Ford Museum you enter a large well lit room and there, on a platform, you see the beautiful shiny latest model of a Ford, the new Thunderbird or LTD, the final product of all these years of innovation and hard work

but here, and I gestured to the space around us, the empty hall where we stood, here you find nothing, a void, an emptiness, a few words scribbled on the walls, this whole machine has led to this, to this vacuum, the whole Nazi machine has produced nothing, nothing but an absence, it was invented to fabricate death

You're right, Hank said, I wonder if they planned this museum with that in mind, in order to give you this sense of emptiness, this feeling of absence when you reach this room, and you know something, he added, it even smells of death in here

we emerged into the yard, the sun was still shining brightly, just above the walls, Miriam was wiping her eyes, Grace Kelly put her sun glasses back on, we stood silent for a while, then the starlet said to me, You mind if I take your picture in front of this building, I would like to have it for my collection, I'll send you a print

Go ahead, I told her, but make sure you get my good side

I think we all felt we had had enough of this place, but Miriam insisted that we should see the memorials up close, so we walked across the entire space of the camp, the Grace Kelly starlet went to the Christian memorial, Hank, Miriam, and I to the Jewish one, it was well done, austere and yet moving,

Miriam bent down and picked up four pebbles from the ground, she placed them on the ledge of the memorial wall, and then softly she said Kaddish

That was for your mother and father and your sisters, she said to me later, somehow she had forced that bit of history out of me while we walked through the museum, But it didn't happen here, I told her, they died at Auschwitz, Oh doesn't matter, she replied, and besides I'll do the same again when I get to Auschwitz next week

she was all right Miriam, I tell you, she was all right with her guilt and her sentimentality, she cared

we left her at the train station in Munich, she wanted to kiss each of us, so I bent down, she was very short, five two or three, and she kissed me on both cheeks, I felt the wet of her eyes, Goodbye Miriam, I said, perhaps we'll meet again in America

Oh that would be so nice, she said, here let me give you my address in Teaneck, and she wrote it neatly on the back of an envelope, If you come I'll fix you some of my delicious Matzo ball soup, and a brisket of beef with Kasha, and for dessert I'll make you some nice cheese cake, my own special recipe

Quite a woman, Hank said, as we hailed a taxi to get back to the hotel, it was late now, the visit had taken the entire day, none of us felt like dinner, we had eaten something standing up at the station in Dachau while waiting for the train, a couple of Würstchen with a mug of that delicious Bavarian beer

How about a nightcap, Hank suggested in the lobby of the hotel, we found a quiet spot in the bar, ordered some schnapps, first time for the starlet, What a day, Hank said, but I'm glad I went, I think it's important to see these things, personally I didn't suffer from the Holocaust, but I know a lot of people whose relatives died here, and in other camps, I want to make a film about all this, we got a script, not a bad one, based in fact on the true story of a survivor, a Jewish woman who stayed alive in Auschwitz, yes I think that was the place, because she played the violin in an orchestra, did you know they had people in the camps who played music for the German officers

Yes, I heard about that, perhaps the only time in history when art saved human lives

the starlet sat quietly, listening to Hank and me talk, What amazes me, Hank was saying, is how carefully they kept records of all that, those pictures after all were taken by the people who ran the camps, what strange need did they have to want to preserve a visual record of these atrocities, doesn't make sense to me

It's a basic human need, I said, a need to keep track of what man supposedly does to perfect history, I'm sure they were convinced that what they were doing was for the good of humanity, they were cleaning up the world of all that filth, that vermin

Yes I suppose it's a matter of how one interprets what is good and what is evil, Hank mused

he was all right too, I was beginning to like him in spite of his Hollywoodish attitude, his phony affectations, and the way he dressed, I only noticed it when we sat in that bar, but he had visited Dachau wearing a plaid sport coat, tight fitting white pants, a baby blue shirt open to the waist, and had a colorful silk scarf loosely tied around his neck, and, oh yes, he wore a pair of suede shoes, white bucks, I don't know why this struck me as incongruous

after a couple of drinks Hank said, Well it's been a long day and it's getting late, tomorrow we want to hit the museums, I understand the Alte Pinakothek is quite something to see, better get a good night's rest, I think I'll go up, you coming Baby

You mind if I sit here a while and talk with our friend, Grace Kelly said, I'm not sleepy yet, I'll have one more drink

Sure, it's okay, but try not to wake me when you come up, and then turning to me and shaking my hand, and what about you, where to from here, have you some plans

Oh, I don't know, I'll bum around, maybe I'll go visit a friend in Switzerland, that sounded like the right thing to say, suddenly it occurred to me that they had no idea who I was, what I was doing, where I came from and where I was going, somehow we had spent two full days together, had shared a profound experience, and yet managed not to reveal anything about ourselves, I'm on vacation, I lied

Well, perhaps we'll see you in the morning for breakfast, we want to get going early, if not, Hank said warmly, good luck to you wherever you go, then he kissed the starlet on the cheek and left

Grace Kelly and I sat for a while in silence, a bit embarrassed to find ourselves alone, she was even more beautiful now in the semi-darkness of the bar than before, Nice fellow, I said

Oh Hank, yes he's wonderful, and he's been so good to me, you can't imagine, without him I would be nothing, I mean I would still be playing bit parts in summer stock, or doing television commercials

I was going to probe further into her life, her ambitions, her desires, when quite unexpectedly she reached for my hand across the table and squeezed it gently, her hand was cold, I was watching you this afternoon, she said, I saw something in your face, something I couldn't quite make out when you were looking at these pictures, were you there

Oh I suppose one could say I was, by extension, we are all survivors

Tell me, please tell me about it, her voice was soft and pleading, and I don't know why but I started telling her the story, you know, that story of the little boy in the closet, the trains rolling in the night, I even told her the story of the raw potatoes

What raw potatoes, Moinous and I asked, we were still sitting at La Coupole drinking our Calvados

Yes, what's that, the raw potatoes, I asked Moinous and Namredef, I never heard that story

Oh you know that story, he said to us, the raw potatoes on the train, I've told it to you so many times before, don't you remember when the kid finally left the closet in his father's overcoat and that big fedora hat on his head, he wandered in the streets of the city, hiding in doorways whenever he saw someone approaching, it was the middle of the night now, he had no idea where to go of course, or what to do, but somehow he found himself in front of the train station, and even he, in his confused twelve-year-old mind, understood that if he could take a train, if he could sneak on a train going anywhere, he might escape this nightmare, so he wandered into the station which was quite busy for this time of night, and noisy, there were lots of people with bags and suitcases, and soldiers everywhere, he stood next to a woman with two children, pretending he was with her, hoping that perhaps he could simply follow her when she boarded the train, but suddenly there was commotion in the station, the soldiers were shouting and pushing the men into a corner of the waiting hall, all the men, and he was among them, in his overcoat that fell to his ankles, still barefoot, and was lined against the wall with the rest of the men, he was tall for his age

an officer ordered the men to drop their pants, and when his turn came he opened his coat, dropped his boy shorts to his feet, remember that's all he was wearing, and exposed his little penis, it was circumcised of course, so they took him too with the rest of the Jews, and later they pushed him into a train, one of those freight cars with a sign that reads, 20 horses or 40 men, it was packed with children, boys, little ones and older ones, only boys, huddled together, the car smelled of urine, and there was a lot of sobbing and crying in there

I'm sure I've told you that story before, in any event the train kept stopping, and then going for a while, and stopping again, that went on for hours, for days, maybe three or four days, nobody knew how long, or in which direction the train was heading, all these kids could think about was food, they had not been given anything to eat since the train left the station, and was it hot in that car, it must have been July, or perhaps August

one night, during a long stop in the middle of nowhere, the boy managed to crawl near to the door by stepping over the bodies of the other boys, and pushed it open a crack, you know those big sliding doors on freight cars, he just sat there sticking his head outside, another boy about his age came and sat next to him but they didn't talk, then a train came from the other direction and stopped on the next track, almost at arm's reach, he pushed the door slightly more, he could hear the soldiers talking but could see no one between the two trains, he looked around, it was not too dark outside, further down, in the next car, he saw another boy, about his size, jump across the tracks and disappear into the second train, so he also jumped across, hung on to the side of the car with one hand while with the other he pushed the door open, it slid easily

Did the other boy who was sitting with him also jump, the starlet asked

No, I don't know why, but he didn't, anyway he went inside that car, it was stacked high with burlap bags full of potatoes, huge muddy potatoes, he climbed on top of the bags, tore one open with his hands, with his nails, took out some of these potatoes, rubbed them against his coat to get the dirt off and started eating

You mean just like that, raw potatoes, the starlet seemed shocked, wow that must taste awful

Yes raw, skin, dirt and all, I don't know how long he sat there eating these potatoes, or how many he ate, he even stuffed some in his coat pockets for later, but he kept chewing and chewing until he felt sick to his stomach, and finally when he couldn't swallow any more, when he felt he was going to throw up, he climbed down from the bags, went to the door to return to his own train, the one with the other boys, but imagine his panic, his fright when he discovered that the train had left, he had been so busy eating his potatoes he hadn't even heard it pull away, what could he do now, he never thought of escaping when he jumped, no, he was only looking for something to eat, hunger had driven him to that train, not the thought of escape, but that's how he survived, how he missed going to the camps

the starlet's eyes were all wet, and when I stopped talking she murmured, Poor little boy, poor little boy, it was you wasn't it

No, I told her, it's just a story, but she wouldn't believe me, she kept repeating, I know it's your story, the way you tell it, has to be your story, she was sitting next to me now and I could feel the warmth of her thigh against mine, and her hand gently stroking my knee

Look, I said to her, that's all it is, a story, anybody's story, one story among millions of others just like it

we sat a while longer in that bar, she was very close to me now, full of emotion and pity, and then, I don't remember when or how, but we were in the elevator, and she had her arms around me, and her mouth was reaching for mine, and of course I had a huge hard-on, Oh I am so sorry, she kept saying between wet kisses, so sorry for you, and then we were in my room, and I remember thinking, Shit what's going on, her hands were touching me, unbuttoning my shirt, unfastening my belt, un-zipping my fly, and she kept whispering, Poor little boy, poor little boy, can you imagine the situation I was in, the bitch wanted to fuck me out of pity

I was getting angry, more and more furious, I felt like kicking her out of my room, but by then we were standing naked in the middle of the floor, our clothes at our feet, holding on to each other passionately, I could see our bodies in the long mirror on the wall behind, I saw my hand grab one of the cheeks of her ass, and what a splendid ass, tight white skin, I watched my hand reach deep between her legs from behind, one of her legs was up, resting on one toe as she pressed her body against mine, she started to groan, her hand was holding on to my cock and squeezing it, rubbing it against her golden pubic hair, I could still see us in the mirror, our two bodies swaying slowly, it suddenly occurred to me that Hank might come bursting through the door and find us like this, start a scandal, a fight, Fuck it, I said to myself, she asked for it

I pushed her toward the bed and fell on top of her, I wanted to screw the hell out of her, but she was soft, gentle, so gentle in fact she made me gentle too, I wasn't fucking her, she was fucking me, with such tenderness, I mean with such compassion, such pity, I was completely disarmed, I tell you she may have been the most gorgeous female I ever screwed in my life, but I was not enjoying it, and yet she stayed a long time, did everything to me, licked me from head to toes, sucked me, screwed me again and again, I felt totally washed out, deflated, and she kept whispering and groaning, I'm coming, I'm coming again, I swear I almost fell asleep in the middle of the whole thing

she left my room a few hours later, got completely dressed, even put on some makeup, I was lying in bed, dumbfounded, exhausted, she kissed me, and then said, Thank you, thank you, you're a marvelous person, I will never forget you

after she left anger came back over me, Who the hell needs her pity, I told myself, I walked around the room like a wild beast in a cage, took a shower, it was past four in the morning, I got dressed, picked up my suitcase full of Deutschmark, left a few bills on the dresser to pay for the room, and walked out of that hotel, even the night porter was asleep on one of the sofas in the lobby, I didn't want to see anyone, especially not them, the movie director and his nymphet

around six o'clock in the morning I caught a train at the station, first one that came along, it was going to Stuttgart and then Basel, Fuck it, I'll go to Basel, anywhere to get the hell out of here

I fell asleep in an empty first class compartment, hours later when I awoke, the train had just pulled in at the Baden-Baden station, Ahah, Baden-Baden, that's where Dostoevsky gambled, sure in 1863, I remember, won a lot of money here, then lost it all, even considered committing suicide in this place, Roulettenburg, as he called it, I jumped off the train just as it was starting to roll

I took a room in the hotel across from the station, slept a few hours, had a good dinner, Schweinekotelett mit Kartoffeln, Gurkensalat, and around nine o'clock that evening, my pockets stuffed with Deutschmark, I walked into the elegant Baden-Baden casino

Dammit, this time I was going all the way, I was going to leave this fucking country rich, take it all back from them

I gambled for two days and two nights straight, I kept running back to my hotel room to get more money out of the suitcase, I was losing, oh not fast, no, they kept teasing me, torturing me, letting me win a hand now and then, hit a corner of a number at the roulette table, un carré, or un cheval, but never a full number, yes I was losing, and I knew it, I kept raising the stakes, I tried baccarat, blackjack, then back to the roulette table, I could feel it getting away from me, and they knew it, oh did they know it, the Germans around the tables, the other gamblers, the two-bit gamblers who were watching me, the voices were soft, the eyes gray, staring at me, and the croupiers were almost smiling with their Nazi faces and their long sticks that kept pulling my money away from me, but I wasn't ready to give in

I ran back to the hotel, perhaps for the sixth time, there'd been a lot of money in that suitcase, but now I took the last handful, everything, and I was back at the roulette table, I must have smoked a good twenty packs of cigarettes during those two days and two nights, lousy German cigarettes, my throat was burning

I put 200 Marks on number four, Einundzwanzig Rot Ungerade und Passieren, the fucking croupier said, twenty-one, right next to the four on the wheel, I had it, finished, I felt like an ass, like a beggar when I placed my last piece, five Marks, on number twenty-two, Monsieur, the croupier said to me in French, le minimum à cette table c'est vingt Mark

the arrogance of that bastard, he and his fellow-croupiers had watched me lose a fortune here and he had the guts to remind me of the minimum, I picked up my five Mark piece and threw it at the croupier across the table, Pour les employés, I shouted, and fuck you, and I walked out of the casino

back in my hotel room, which I had paid for in advance, I stretched on the bed, kicked the empty suitcase into a corner of the room, I stared at the ceiling, Idiot, imbecile, I said aloud, but it was too late, they had taken everything, everything away from me

I was looking at the chandelier, a massive, rococo monstrosity, all brass, enormous, with little angels holding up the light bulbs, I counted them, thirty-six, and then I decided, this is it, what the hell, why not end it all here, this is as good a place as any other, maybe I was destined to end here, I got up, pulled the sheets off the bed, twisted them tight into a rope, climbed on a chair and pulled at the chandelier several times with all my strength, it seemed solid, anything German is solid, I tied one end of my rope to it, made a loop with the other end and passed it around my neck, can you guys visualize me standing there on that chair in that richly decorated room, in Baden-Baden, I had even written a suicide note, you won't believe this, the last words of Dostoevsky's The Gambler, Tomorrow, tomorrow it will all come to an end

I kicked the chair away and the rope pulled at my neck, and then everything cracked, I was flat on my back on the floor, half of the ceiling came crashing down on top of me, I had plaster and dust in my eyes and in my mouth, the damn chandelier hit me in the stomach, there were scratches and bruises all over my face, how ridiculous can a man be people passing in the hallway outside my room must have heard the ceiling crashing, and the sound my body made when it hit the floor, I heard them calling the manager, and a few moments later he appeared in the room with the maids, the servants, the doorman all crowded behind him, and more faces trying to squeeze in the doorway, and there I was sprawled on the floor, still half dazed, with that enormous chandelier resting across my stomach, plaster and debris of the ceiling all over me

no one smiled or laughed, oh no, they just stared at me with their German gaze, they even looked concerned, then two or three of them helped me up, brushed off my clothes while apologizing to me, I pushed them aside, I'm all right, I'm okay, I kept saying, leave me alone, and I walked out of the room, ran down the stairs and out into the street, I left the suitcase behind of course, it was empty now

Goddammit, I can't even die in this fucking country, no, they won't let me die here

Well, that's the whole story, you guys wanted to know what I did, now you know, after that I found a way to get to Paris where I've been for the past few months, surviving as best I can, hustling those dumb pimps at billiards, trying to put myself back together

You're amazing, you know, we said to him, you're mad, why the hell do you do that to yourself, what's wrong with you, why can't you forget the past and go on like a normal human being

we had left the Coupole and were walking down Rue de Rennes toward his hotel, it was quite late now, the streets were deserted, we arrived in front of his hotel, a fleabag, Rue Jacob, Hôtel des Deux Continents, Moinous noticed, how perfectly ironic

Oh I know the place, I cut in, I stayed there once, years ago, yes Rue Jacob, down the street from Les Editions du Seuil, how appropriate for him, Hôtel des Deux Continents

That's right, Namredef confirmed

You two want to come up for a minute, the old man asked, it's not much of a place but what can you expect

we walked up the narrow stairs to the third floor, there was a sharp smell of overcooked cauliflower in the staircase, No it was the smell of rancid piss, Moinous corrected Namredef, Okay the smell of piss if you prefer

the room was tiny, barely large enough for the bed, a table and one chair, a touch of naturalism here on the part of Namredef

Make yourselves comfortable if you can find room where to sit, il faut que j'aille pisser un coup, the old man said as he walked down the half-flight of stairs to the W.C.

You mean to say the room had no toilet, I inquired

Are you kidding, Moinous answered, a private pissoir in a dump like that

the two of us sat on the edge of the bed, we were beginning to feel the excitement of the day in our bones, Stop yawning, I said to Moinous who seemed ready to flop on the bed, it's not polite

Dammit, it's not my fault, I'm bushed, I can't keep my eyes open

Me too I'm exhausted, but aren't you glad we found him

Yes, of course, but why do we have to stick around tonight, it's so late, why can't we come back tomorrow

No, I don't think we should leave him, not tonight, he needs us

we glanced around the room, what a mess, the sheets of the unmade bed looked and smelled like they hadn't been changed in weeks, dirty clothes and crumpled pieces of paper all over the

floor, a T-shirt, one pair of Eminence shorts and two un-
matched socks were drying on the radiator like dead fish, once
you fall into naturalism it's not easy to get out of it, in a corner a
pile of old newspapers, a few abused books here and there,
some open to the page where he had stopped reading, I picked
up one of the books just to see what the old man was reading
these days, Spengler, The Decline of the West, hmm, interesting, next to the typewriter on the table a moldy loaf of pain de
campagne and an open box of stale camembert, on the bare wall
a snapshot held by a thumbtack, nothing else, it was an old
photograph of the three of us, the old man standing in the
middle, tall and slim in a gray suit, and the two of us, Moinous
and I, at his sides, small round and chubby like two balls, from
where we sat on the bed, the three of us in that picture looked
like the sculpture of a giant phallus in erection and a pair of
testicles, though somewhat blurred against a landscape of trees
and a piece of white cloud, but from another angle we looked
like a rocketship, yes like a spaceship pointing skyward with
two fuel tanks attached to its sides

This picture has great symbolic possibilities, Moinous remarked when I pointed it out to him, but neither he nor I could
recall when and where it had been taken

When you think of those two assholes with their knives up their
sleeves and you look at this stinking place, the old man said
when he returned from the toilet still buttoning his fly, you
realize how right the guy was who said, I forget his name, some
historian, who said in 1899, France is tragically unprepared for
the 20th century, how prophetic he was, well one could say that
France is now comically unprepared for the 21st century, he sat
at the table, facing us, he looked like a professor getting ready to
lecture to his class, he pushed aside some papers

we didn't speak for a while, Moinous and I were a bit uneasy,
the old man had closed his eyes, but he was not asleep, his
fingers were drumming the table, finally I asked pointing to the
snapshot on the wall, Tell me where did you get that picture

Oh that thing, don't you remember, it was taken in Central

Park, in New York, the day they awarded me the Frances Steloff Prize, in 19, shit I forget the year, 1971, wasn't it, what a joke that was

I don't think he was right about the date and the place, but I wasn't sure myself, and besides I was just trying to make conversation

How about a drink, he said suddenly as he knelt on the floor and pulled out two bottles of cheap Nicolas wine from under the bed, we took turns drinking directly from the bottle, Moinous and I delicately, somewhat reluctantly, but the old man put away half a bottle in two gulps, we had never known him to drink like this, not him, on the contrary, always preaching sobriety, it was obvious from the look on our faces that we were concerned

Ah the drunken days and the vomitous nights that run together into a sleepless blur, he said wiping his mouth with the back of his hand, sometimes it's necessary you know, he kicked the empty bottle across the floor, But I suppose you guys want to know what I've been doing the past few months, eh, well in a way I've been asking myself in this shithole if we are capable of a radical interrogation, I'm serious, that's what I've been doing, or if you prefer, I've been asking myself if as a last resort we are still capable of literature, not an easy question my friends, no not an easy question, but that's what I've been doing in this merdier littéraire du sixième arrondissement, what a fucking circus this place is, bordel de tous les bordels, he took another gulp of wine from the bottle, But you know something, without the idea of free will the human race is of no interest at all, and that is the real problem today, free will, and certainly without free will there can be no literature, and then he told us about the novel he had just finished, he sounded happy now, happy to be with us again, and we were too

You won't believe this, but I worked on the damn thing for seven months, yes seven months straight, night and day, 15 hours, 18 hours at a time, almost went nuts in this crummy room, this stinking closet, banging away on that old selectric of mine, he passed his hand sensuously on top of the typewriter in front of him

I see you still have that old machine of yours, Moinous remarked

Yeah, can't get rid of it, still balling away with it, almost went bananas here, banging my head against the wall, but now it's finished, yes finished, done, would you like to know what it is, there was a glimmer of excitement in his eyes, he stroked his beard with his hand, Let me put it this way, instead of turning old dreams into history I've been converting history into dreams, into nightmares rather, yes, do you remember that line from William Blake, Fire delights in its form, well that's what I've been doing, turning my inner fire, or whatever else you want to call those squeaks in my guts, into pure form, might be the best stuff I've ever written, I'm serious, really I'm not snowing you, but who knows, ah well, doesn't matter anyway

Oh I'm sure it's good, Moinous said while I also approved with my head, the last thing of yours we read was already quite something, what was it called, Amer, Amer something, oh yes Amer Eldorado, what a mad delirious book that was, but what's this new one about

Hey, why don't I read it to you, I mean the new book, it's only twenty pages long, it won't take too long

I thought you said it was a novel, we exlaimed somewhat surprised

Yes a twenty page novel, what's wrong with that, not all novels need to go on forever, and anyway you'll see each page is like twenty pages of normal writing, I mean it, it's so condensed, only the essential has remained, yes the essential, everything else was flushed down the toilet, all the superfluous verbiage, not a word too much, just a long syntactical disarticulation, without beginning or end, as it should be, but in the right place,

I hope, yes just words, words abandoned to deliberate chaos and yet boxed into an inescapable form, you'll see, boxes of words

we were puzzled of course, and though it was quite late now and we were exhausted, we said, Okay go ahead, read it to us

he pulled out a messy manuscript from a cardboard box under the bed, sat at the table, put on his reading glasses, It's like a cry, he said, a long cry, but not of despair, no, just a cry

he cleared his throat, It's called The Voice in the Closet, he said as he flipped over the first page, and then he began to read in a quick deep tone of voice never lifting his eyes from the pages

Wow, what a reading, what a story, you should have heard him, Namredef said to me, we were overwhelmed, we didn't know what to say at first, we just sat there dumbfounded

Well, what do you think, you guys like it, he asked as he put away his manuscript, I'm really excited about this piece, seven months I worked on the damn thing, seven months for twenty pages

It's fantastic, really tremendous, we said in a single voice, perhaps a bit obscure, and not easy to follow, especially toward the end, the last pages, the last gasp, but it's very moving, we added quickly, also it's reminiscent of that story you told us in Palermo, remember, about the little boy in the closet who has to take a shit and wraps it in a newspaper and then puts the package on the roof, or at least it sounds like another version of that story

Well somewhat, all stories are the same, but never mind the story, what do you think of the writing, the flow of the language, the form, that's what concerns me, I don't give a shit about the story, and what do you mean when you say it's not easy to follow, what the hell does that mean, don't you understand that it's the only way this story could be written, I had to do it this way, it's a demanding subject for which a demanding form had to be invented

No, that's not what we mean, really it's a great piece of writing, we were not putting you down, certainly one of the best pieces you've ever written, one of the most unusual too, but it's heavy going, hard to follow, you know, takes a lot of concentration, maybe it's because the two of us are so tired, and

You old farts don't understand a damn thing, think of the madness of sketching all these possible words into an appropriate form, the desire and the need to add more, the excitement of chance too, but also think of the cool restraint, the control, the necessary calculation, to the point of counting the number of letters in words to justify their presence, or their elimination, think of the extreme reserve and the cunning, ah yes the cunning that such a game presupposes, because you see the controlled poignancy of the language is intended to guard against the emotional sway of the submerged drama

Irrational balance, Namredef said

Okay, pure madness, but between this madness and this caution each word must be written, set down as though it were the last one, yes the last gasp, standing on the edge of a precipice leaning against the wind, and the one word that happens to have no successor can only be the last one for just a moment

Exercise in diminishing endlessness in other words, Namredef replied while Moinous scratched his head and mumbled in a distorted echo, Or augmenting infiniteness

Ah fuck you, both of you, you guys are really tightassed, dammit, don't you see, it is this last moment, neither more nor less ultimate than the others which carries the game to its highest point of intensity, for it is this last moment that the writer has chosen at his own risk to cancel the story, to turn away from it, and let the ruins of memories unfold in their uninterrupted glory

Ah shit, that's all you're interested in, form, form and semantic games, but what about the content, yes what about the story of the little boy in the closet, what about the Jews, the camps, the gas chambers, the final solution, why the hell don't you come out with it

It's all there, you schmucks, inside the words, teller and told, survivors and victims unified into a single design, if you read the text carefully then you'll see appear before you on the shattered white space the people drawn by the black words, flattened and disseminated on the surface of the paper inside the black inkblood, that was the challenge, never to speak the reality of the event but to render it concrete into the blackness of the words

That's a lot of bullshit, Namredef argued back, yes balls, foutaise and excrement, and there is plenty of it in your story, though I must admit I rather like the image of the package full of shit on the roof, nice symbolic gesture when the kid places it up there, also that busy sexy selectricstud of yours is quite a character, it has a liberating quality in its frantic movements

It's useless to discuss literature with you, you guys don't want to understand a damn thing, it's precisely the fact of the physical text that promises a potential freedom, the closet exists only as a sequence of squares, of doors if you prefer, just as the voices in the text exist only as a sequence of cries, the voices can be extended beyond the text into history, but one can never find the door that leads to the origin or the end of the little boy's story, the selectricstud merely humps paper within the great cunt of existence, and that's the ultimate irony of this sequestration, the reason it had to be written this way

That's quite obvious, Moinous said, but that machine of yours seems to be enjoying it, and that's why it remains a game

You guys are shits, you really know how to make a friend feel good, you're a bunch of crumbs, he walked over to the window and looked outside, his back turned to us, it was almost daylight

Well, I suppose we'd better get going and get some sleep, we said, we'll talk some more tomorrow

What do you mean, he turned around, you're not going to leave me alone, not now, you're crazy, stay here, we'll manage somehow, please stay, here I'll sleep on the floor and you two can share the bed

No no, come on, we can't do that, deprive you of your bed, and besides you must be exhausted

Don't argue, he spread a blanket on the floor and stretched on it without even undressing, face down, his right arm bent under his head as a pillow, You see it's fine, stop yapping now and go to sleep, he said as he kicked his shoes away, we'll talk tomorrow

Namredef and Moinous undressed, down to their colorful boxer shorts, and crawled into the bed, Moinous next to the wall, Namredef on the outside, Don't cross this line Moimoi or I'll kick your butt, Namredef said as he brought his arm down in the center of the bed along an imaginary line, Ah shut up and let me sleep, Moinous grumbled

soon they heard the old man snoring on the floor, Are you asleep, Namredef asked Moinous, No I can't fall asleep, I'm too worked up

Me too, what a night, and then after a moment of silence, Hey Moimoi, what did you think of his voice in the closet, quite something eh

Yes, but I think he's going to have problems getting it published, who the hell wants to read something that confused, and that unreadable too, this time he really went too far, hey Nam, do you think we were too hard on him, that perhaps we should have

No, I don't think so, what else could we have said, one must always be honest with friends they each turned to one side, ass to ass in the narrow bed, the old man was still snoring on the floor, Moinous, goddammit, move your fat ass, you're taking up all the room

I'm trying but this fucking bed is so small, and so hard too, a few minutes passed, then all of a sudden Namredef sat upright in bed, You know I think he's wrong about that picture on the wall, it was not taken when he said, if you look at it carefully you'll see that we are much too young for 1971, it was taken much before that, in fact I believe it goes way back to the days when we were members of the Workmen's Circle, remember, when the three of us

I don't give a shit about the picture, Moinous replied pulling the blanket over his head, and fuck the Workmen's Circle, let me sleep, dammit, you have no consideration for anybody

Namredef turned away from Moinous and closed his eyes, outside in the street the garbage collectors were clanking the cans, but now the three of them were asleep in that tiny room, it was never reported however if they dreamt or not, though one can assume they did, perhaps they even had the same dream, with slight variations of course

they were good friends, old friends, from the beginning, and still are, the three of them, The Three Musketeers of Surfiction, they were called, way back then, when they were at the forefront of the literary avant-garde, experimenting with all sorts of wild subversive narrative techniques, Gimmicks, the critics would sneer, Well let them sneer, the old man would say whenever he came across one of those parasitic remarks, rira bien qui rira le dernier

and now he wants us to leave him alone in that antechamber of departure, sitting on his metallic box which contains the last scraps of his life, dammit, time is running out, and we haven't progressed at all

Leave me alone, he tells us, leave me now, he repeated softly, not with sadness, nor with anger, I have to gather myself

Gather yourself, you'll have lots of time for that out there in space

yes I suppose, before the dememorization process, that's what they call it, when they empty your head of all memories, soon after the spaceship is en route, after the initial leap, when the deportees are spaceborne, so I'm told, that's what they do, dememorize you, soon after the briefing stage, so that once you've departed you can be mentally recycled for the colonies, those bastards, they plug your head into some electronic gadget which cleans your brain of all earthly connections

VII

Never mind the futuristic crap in this final account, yes definitely I'll skip the pseudoscientific gimmicks, no gadgetry, as I said, but nonetheless some realistic details are essential if we are to situate ourselves properly in time and not give in to desperate preminiscences, after all this is the real thing, a search for the truth, so to speak, and we are the ultimate witnesses, last to stand by him, with him in his earthly closet, last to question, to challenge the reasons for his expulsion, however unfounded these may be, there must be a justifiable explanation for his number to have come up, just as this old century comes to an end, curious coincidence, and we stand on the threshold of the century of hope

Hope my ass, Namredef interjects

we are sitting in my study, in front of my typewriter, an old I.B.M. selectric, we are in progress, somehow we'll get to the end of this matter, unless something unexpected occurs, teller and told expelled from reality into an intangible world, exiled into fictional illusions, and where without ceasing to be inside we see ourselves from the outside, triple-headed creature who forces his twin-self to vanish behind him, or rather before him, and yet still hoping, still working for a solution

Hope, what a joke, Moinous joins in, hope itself is an illusion fostered by the very powers that are denying our undertaking, whether we like it or not we are cornered in a labyrinth of deceptions, we have lost our sense of communion with the past, feel no responsibility for the future, and have been rendered purposeless, directionless, by our own digressive discourse

Hold it Moinous, I say, what's going on, I don't get it

No, let me continue, I've got to get this off my chest, our complacency toward the chaotic condition of our plotless existence and its lack of dramatic development, our acquiescence in the rules of fictional bureaucracy, as well as our acceptance of the corruption of life into a performance provide us with the evidence that what we have given up was better than what we have got instead, we are hopelessly disengaged from history and yet prisoner of our own narcissistic story

Phew, I had no idea you were that dissatisfied with our present situation, why didn't you speak up sooner

Wait, I'm not finished, convinced that there is nothing to question but the question itself, like nightingales singing endlessly in the dark, we have rendered the theory of questioning compatible with the practice of inhumanity, but perhaps we should stop questioning questioning and start asking questions about society and our role in it, and as he speaks these words Moinous turns to Namredef asking for his approval with a motion of the head, right there in front of me, the two of them, inside my own words, what's going on

Well I'll be damned, this kind of talk will not get us anywhere, on the contrary, it will make us regress rather than progress, that's for sure, but tell me Moinous, what about history, the lessons of history, and what about sociology, not to mention cultural and political radicalism, don't you think these can still provide some answers, no my dear Moinous, I will not give in to your easy despair and pessimism

Oh yes, what about history and sociology, what about your phony cultural and political radicalism, don't make me laugh Federman, the political crisis of our evasive bureaucratic powers reflects a general crisis in Western culture which reveals itself in a pervasive despair of ever understanding the course of modern history or of subjecting it to a rational direction, history is bankrupt, didn't you know that, and so is sociology, bankrupt, as for cultural radicalism, it merely seems to attack the status quo, but in fact it supports it unwittingly because in exposing objective reason as an ideology, radicalism leaves itself no means of legitimizing its own critique of injustice, exploitation, and of course realism, well I am fed up with that kind of condition, fed up also with your compulsory optimism, I want out of here

it is not often that Moinous allows himself such diatribes, but I suppose the situation is getting to him, its hopelessness, its sinuousness, It's true, I say, searching for some way to reassure him and make him persist, that it is in vain that the Western world seeks for itself a form of agony worthy of its past, nonetheless one must have the courage of one's narcissism, one must continue to survive even in the midst of the incredible obscenity of human monotony and words of despair will not resolve the situation at hand, what we need now is action, don't give up on me you guys, we'll find a way out of here, I promise you, we'll save that old man one way or another

Action, yes, action will perhaps get us out of this dilemma, Namredef butts in from his corner, but there is some truth in what Moinous is saying, we do live our lives with a sense of inner emptiness, boundless repressed rage and frustration, and unsatisfied oral cravings, we're not blaming you, but look how calculating and devious we have become, doesn't make sense any more, notice also the decline of the spirit of play in us, the deteriorating relations between us, and then tell us that there is still hope, that everything is fine, that eventually our undertaking will turn out for the best, who are you kidding

Will you two grouches stop, dammit, what's going on here,

you're sabotaging my system, but they ignore me completely and turn away, indifferent to my voice, beyond the reach of my fingers, and they go on complaining and gesticulating like two mechanical toys, two mindless robots powered by remote control, I'm so disgusted I'm ready to dump them right here, and the whole damn story too

we are still sitting in my study, sulking at each other, cornered into an impasse of futility and disaccord when suddenly, after a long uncomfortable pause, Namredef says, Perhaps what we need now is a symbolic gesture, a symbolic breakthrough

Yes, that would help a great deal, Moinous adds addressing me directly, what we need now is a solution beyond the final solution of realism, our old man should do something, something revealing, doesn't have to be too extravagant or earthshaking, but something, I mean for instance like what Henry James did in 1899

And what the hell was that, I inquire

On new year's eve 1899, so I am told, Henry James shaved his beard, do you realize what that means, it means that the entire course of history, well recent history at any rate, was dramatically altered by that gesture, the disappearance of that arcadian beard, no that glorious cosmopolitan beard, to use the correct terms, from the landscape of literary history opened the door, in reverse motion one might say, to all sorts of symbolic and hermeneutic possibilities, I don't think we have yet fully realized the importance of that act of self-defacement, in my opinion, the fact that Henry James calculatingly shaved his beard, just as the 19th century was coming to an end, is as important, as enlightening, metaphorically speaking, as the appearance, at about the same time, of the Eiffel Tower in the middle of Paris, yes as important, in terms of historical simultaneity, as the rising of that great phallic symbol in the landscape of Western civilization, one must never underestimate such a coincidence, especially now

Too bad our old man no longer sports a beard, Namredef deplores, he did once, you may recall, but shaved it in 1994, and not as a dramatic or a symbolic gesture, no, Never again, he said, it itches too much, perhaps he too could change the course of history, or at least reverse it, and thus save himself if he were to grow a beard now

I never thought of that, it could work, I say as I visualize in my mind our old man gently stroking an imaginary white beard

Even a false beard might work, Moinous suggests, why don't we try, let's bring him a false beard and see what happens

No, that would be too obvious, too detectable, it would have to be a real beard, I emphasize, except that it takes time, weeks, to grow a beard, I mean a substantial beard, and we are running out of time, especially since we have been wasting so much of it sitting here, helpless, contemplating our failures, and all you guys can tell me is that he is still waiting in that antechamber of departure, beardless and resigned, waiting for midnight, for the coming of the new year that will launch him into space, all you can tell me is that he refuses to say anything, do anything to save himself, No, leave me alone, close the door behind you, this is what he said, according to you when you last saw him a few hours ago and left him there sitting on that metallic box of his

Which contains, supposedly, Namredef interrupts, the last scraps of his life, a few old books, some faded photographs, his private papers and manuscripts, I'm only guessing of course

And no doubt a complete set of his published works, Moinous adds, not much indeed

Nevertheless a whole life, Namredef says bitterly, reduced to a pile of yellowed sheets of paper to be dumped into orbit

Look you guys, let's not go into a useless inventory here, we are not ready yet for a summation

Okay, but that's what he said to us, Close the door behind you, leave me alone

But we just wanted to say goodbye, pay our last respects, we said dejectedly as we left the antechamber

So what did you do after that

We decided to go and speak to the authorities, as a final resort

And what did they tell you

No, Gentlemen, he is not being sent to the colonies, notice how the term deported is never used by the authorities, to the space colonies for racial or religious reasons, nor because of his radical political activities, or his disruptive literary affiliations, certainly not, or because of his sexual, how shall I say, his sexual exuberance, all that is known about him, it is not that unusual, on the contrary, quite normal for our time, as for his optimism, excuse me if I smile, but that's really far-fetched, or his anal compulsion, not at all, we are beyond such banalities, why then, you ask, this is not the place for such inquiries, you have to look elsewhere, here we merely keep files, and let me assure you there is nothing unusual in this case, we attend to Onsela-couledouce, not an easy task, Gentlemen, as you can imagine, especially these days when the very terms of our existence can be so easily converted into the terms of its refutation, as appears to be the case more specifically with your friend's own existence

Is it that bad, we said

Oh not that bad, let's not exaggerate, it's just that, you see, Gentlemen, our ethic and aesthetic speculations with respect to our survival in this world are engaged in a tightrope act in which the significance that must be ascribed to these speculations in order to justify our well-being has to be eliminated so that their authenticity can be guaranteed

Ah, that's how it is, well thank you Ma'am, thank you very much, you've been most helpful and most gracious, we greatly appreciate that, and please excuse us for being so insistent, we had no idea the situation was that complex, goodbye then, you've clarified a lot of things for us, we shall not bother you any more

Do you think we should have probed further, Moinous asked Namredef as they left the Central Office of Onselacouledouce

No, I think we went as far as we could with that, further questioning could have led us into trouble

You know something Nam, what she said made sense, she's a bright woman, and quite charming, though I'm not sure she stated it the right way, it seemed a bit unclear to me, didn't you get confused

Not me, I never get confused, on the contrary, because, as I've told you before, what is said is never really said since it can always be said another way, so you see, it was quite clear, and besides what she said seemed rather superficial to me

damn those two narrators, one never gets anywhere with them, and so once again we have reached an impasse as the three of us remain stranded in the middle of our undertaking, stalled words in regress, here in front of my desk

out of boredom Moinous is practicing endless Schubert Lieder on the old piano in my study with the metronome marking time in the background, he is not bad, while Namredef, totally disgusted, is playing solitaire in a corner of the room mumbling to himself, cursing life in general and his own in particular, and me, out of despair, I'm doing finger exercises on the typewriter, now is the time for all good men to come to the help of their country, now is the time, ninety words a minute, now is the time for all good men, I would have made a great secretary for some high-class executive, now is the time

Hey, I have an idea you guys, I finally say after hours of painful shiftlessness, how about trying to get a clue from the old man, I mean why not go to the spaceport and ask him to show you his notice of convocation, or his travel orders, he must have such documents, in this pragmatic world of ours nothing is done without the proper written records, maybe something revealing will show up, what can we lose, let's try instead of sitting here like vegetables, and then we can work our way back to the present

That's a great idea, Namredef says sweeping his deck of cards onto the floor with the back of his hand, yes, let's project ourselves forward at random, let's explore the situation from a future angle, so far we have been digging into the past, more or less rationally, questioning his past from the reverse of farness, and not too successfully at that, but perhaps the clue lies in the future, or even in the conditional, in the unknown, and as he speaks these words Namredef walks over to where the cards are spread on the floor, kneels, raises one hand in a gesture of astonishment, Holy smoke, you guys won't believe this but I have just lined up, by pure chance, with a wild throw of the cards, a royal flush in spades, and in perfect order, incredible, it must mean something, don't you think so, I tell you it's a sign

Come on Namredef, this is not the time to play games of chance, I say, that won't get us anywhere

Why not, so far we've not been that lucky, why can't we let chance guide our steps for a change

Oh no, royal flush or no royal flush, I will not allow chance to determine our course of action, nor will I allow connotation to assume the objective mask of denotation, not here

Tremendous idea, Moinous jumps up from the piano, yes absolutely, let's explore the future retrospectively, after all we don't have to move in one direction only, why can't we backtrack forwardly, or fortuitously, as Nam suggests, though it is true that the arrow of time, to use that marvelous phrase of Sir Arthur Eddington's, points in an obvious direction, and is aimed toward the future, away from the irretrievable past, which permits us to recognize which way time flows and how we flow with it, and thus we take considerable comfort, for

instance, in our confidence that the carefully arranged marriage
of gin and vermouth is not going to be suddenly annulled in our
glass leaving us with two layers of warm liquid and a lump of
ice, of demelting ice at the bottom of our glass, and a lump of
anguish deep in our throat, but it doesn't have to be this way,
not at all, who says that the rules which govern the movement
of time are absolute, it is a curious fact of nature that the laws
that provide the basis for our understanding of fundamental
physical and biological processes, and presumably fictional
processes as well, do not favor one direction of time's arrow
over another, they would represent the world just as well if
time were flowing backward instead of forward and martinis
were coming apart rather than being created, I mean rather
than being mixed forwardly into some tastefully unified entity,
I tell you that's the answer to our predicament, inverted motion

Hey wait a minute Moinous, don't get carried away, Namredef
cuts in, all we're being asked to do is go and talk to the old man
again, check some documents, move forward a bit, I didn't
mean to suggest that we should run the whole film, the entire
scenario backward as if we were in some kind of television
commercial, I don't see the point of that, next you'll have us
moving obliquely and in slow motion

No let me explain what I'm saying, it might help us proceed
more efficiently and with less anxiety, and certainly in a less
chancy manner than with your accidental royal flush, you see
the asymmetry of the basic laws of nature with respect to the
direction of the flow of time has long been an unstable principle
of physics, Eddington himself dealt with that question at considerable length in his Gifford Lectures of 1927, and he concluded by saying that the laws of nature are indifferent as to a
direction in time, there is no more distinction between past and
future than between right and left in the jungles of nature or in
the great void of space, so why not take advantage of this
instead of going the same old way over and over again

Where the hell are you taking us Moinous, I'm completely lost,
Namredef says apparently disoriented, I've never heard anything more confusing, but tell me Moimoi, since when have

you been so interested in experiments in time reversal, I had no idea

Since always, and besides I'm interested in everything, you should know that, after all the years you and I have been together, everything, and it doesn't matter to me if it makes sense or not, because in my opinion there is as much value in making nonsense as there is in making sense, it's just a matter of direction, forward, backward, sideways, up or down, who cares, what I'm looking for is a way out of this damn thing, any which way will do fine for me, even assbackward, as long as we keep moving and get to the end

Okay Moinous, I understand how you feel, I squeeze in, but still I don't see how this theory of yours is going to help us

It is not my theory, I'm only reporting here, paraphrasing as best I can

That may be so but if anything that kind of theory will land us for sure into a science-fiction situation, and that would be disastrous, yes land us squarely into some inextricable time loop in the style of Stanislaw Lem, and then we'll really be screwed up, all twisted, all turned around inside duplications and triplications of identities, which is what I've been trying to avoid all along, oh no my dear fellows, absolutely not, no sci-fi trappings here

And what's wrong with science-fiction, look at us, what's so realistic about us, Moinous retorts sneeringly, yes look at us stranded on the edge of that extemporaneous precipice of yours, here I am all converged in my name, and Namredef reversed in his, do you think that makes us more realistic, more vraisemblables, who do you think you're fooling with your twofold vibration

Dammit, let's not go into that, I will not allow you to drag me into tautological disjunctures, not in this story

Why not, what are you afraid of, go ahead, we're interested to know why you're shying away from futuristic illusionism, it might be our only salvation since everything else so far has failed

You guys are really something else, why do you insist on pushing me in that direction, don't you know that most science-fiction tends lamentably toward unconvincing futuristic descriptions and explications of the impossible, and usually offsets these unsustainable enormities with simplistic characters and melodramatic plots which animate elementary didacticism, is that what you want, well not here, not in this story, I won't fall for that crap, though that may already be our essential difficulty, the way you are behaving, the way you are conducting your investigation and reporting the facts one would think you believe yourselves in some old-fashioned science-fiction story à la Bradbury, our old man is doomed for sure if we allow ourselves to continue in this vein

That's your fault, you're the one in charge here, why don't you relax, relax and let things follow their natural course and see what develops, especially now that we are on the verge of forging ahead

That would really be a mess, it would certainly make us tumble into infantilism, and if you want my honest opinion the fundamental weakness of most science-fiction, there are of course a few exceptions, some quite remarkable, but I'm not going to give you a bibliography here, the fundamental weakness is that it presumes an incredible amount of innocence and ignorance on the part of its characters once they are launched into the mystery of the universe, as if these characters had never themselves been exposed to any kind of fictional situation, and therefore knew nothing of time warps and time loops, spatial lapses and displacements, theories of stochasticity, and such things, all these dumb characters who float in space can do is play with their futuristic plastic gizmos that look like swollen kitchen utensils, well not in this story, I can assure you, which begins, quite credibly, in the year 2000, or just before, as already established, and frankly the only thing now that can screw up our system is the Apocalypse

The Apocalypse, both Namredef and Moinous look bewildered

Yes, the Apocalypse, what did you expect, and that would really be something, but don't kid yourselves, the possibility looms on the horizon of our near future, especially with all these doomsday kooks warning that unbelievable disasters are roaring down upon us like a whirlwind from the outer limits of the universe, I'm reporting this directly from a recent article in Transuniversal Newsweek, and as a matter of fact many of these doomsday fanatics are already preparing themselves for such an eventuality, digging eternal shelters deep into the Rocky Mountains, under the Pacific Ocean floor, or simply in their basements, as the year 2000 approaches, the article goes on saying, once again they discern in current events the biblical signs foreshadowing the end of the world and the second coming of Christ, shit that's all we need

That would certainly put an end to our story, Moinous interrupts, but we are not there yet because, as you know, the 21st century does not begin until

Yes yes, I am aware that logically the 21st century only begins on the 1st of January, 2001, but in this story, for the convenience of the narrative, we will assume that it begins on January 1st, 2000, in order to coincide in a twofold manner with the eventual departure of our old man and the possible Apocalypse

In other words, not the second coming but the second parting, Namredef suggests without a trace of irony

In a sense yes, one might say that, though our story would really be a mess, regardless of the date, if these apocalyptic fundamentalists were to be right, can you imagine our old man riding away into space on a white horse, what a phony ending that would make

Phony perhaps, but it may be the only ending that would make sense in this case, Moinous says contemplatively

I hope not, but meanwhile these stubborn religious freaks insist that it's coming, and indeed, as our century dwindles away, they are attracting millions of fearful believers through public speeches, movies, tapes, articles, comic strips, and cheap pseudoprophetic novels, but be that as it may, or as it will be, we cannot concern ourselves with such unfounded potential tragic events if we are to continue what we have started and bring it to a satisfactory conclusion, a proper ending, no that would be too fatalistic on our part

And too pessimistic also, Moinous and Namredef add, and besides we would never know what happened to our old man, and why he is being deported to the space colonies

Quite right, and that is why it seems practical to me to have chosen 1994 for the birth of these colonies, even though that date may seem somewhat arbitrary, but chronologically it follows the establishment of world government in 1993, though that too need not be precise or verifiable, it's history now

Don't you think you're pushing this a bit too far now, Moinous remarks

No I am not, you guys are really narrow-minded, you have no sense of historical possibilities, just let me go on, don't you see I'm all worked up by the fever of creation, I'm getting to the heart of this matter, just a little more of an effort and we'll make a breakthrough

Okay, go ahead, but do we have to stick around, why can't we go on with our investigation, why can't we go talk to the old man, as you suggested earlier, while you're trying to get us out of this impasse and put things in order back here

Fine with me, see you guys later, but remember, time is running out, that old man of ours must be saved, so hurry back, I'm just going to straighten out a few things around here, look at my notes, and when you get back we'll decide what to do, if there is still time

Okay, goodbye, we're going now, we're on our way to see the old man, and this time we're not coming back without a clue

phew, they are gone, finally, wow those two bums know how to drag their feet, I hope this time they come back with some concrete facts, meanwhile let's go on with what I was saying

well, that's when the United States of Planet Earth, U.S.P.E., as they are called in this story, were founded, in 1993, predictably enough, and all national boundaries were abolished, and as a result the world became, on the surface at least, a better place in which to live, in which to work, travel, reflect, love, and play also, since life now, daily social and natural life was equally divided between collective sharing and self-gratification

sounds great, you can believe it, more will be said about all that, about daily life in the new United Planet Earth, but let me just state for the time being that what permitted the creation of U.S.P.E. was a burst of laughter, yes a totally unexpected international planetwide outburst of hilarity

suddenly, even though the causes still remain obscure but the effects are quite visible, on April 13, 1993, a Friday in fact, people all over the world started laughing, well if not laughing out loud at least smiling, smiling in the midst of the most serious, even the most horrendous situation, smiling even while frowning which up to then was considered physically and anatomically impossible

suddenly, all over the world people of all races, blacks, whites, yellows, were walking around or standing around with huge grins on their faces, in the streets of the cities, of the villages, in the solitude of nature, in the still partly uncivilized jungles of Africa and Australia, in the coal mines of West Virginia and of the Rhineland, in the Detroit factories, in the schools, the kindergardens, the universities, the great centers of learning, in the drugstores, the department stores, the supermarkets, the offices, the skylabs, in public places and private homes, even in the insane asylums, the prisons, the ghettos, the Siberian gulags, everywhere people exploded into laughter, some madly and uncontrollably, some reservedly, shyly, Japanese style, tittering behind their hands, others more openly while slapping themselves on the belly, and others insolently while urinating in their undergarments, everybody was touched, little girls were giggling delightfully all over the place while little boys were rolling on the ground half choking with effrontery in their boisterous jollity, everybody was involved, the old, the senile, the young, the middle-aged, the teenagers, the infants in their cribs, it was contagious, it even spread into the animal kingdom, monkeys and birds were seen giggling in the trees, zoos became gardens of mirthfulness, domestic and wild life was reunited in laughter

suddenly everybody was taking laughter seriously, at first it was thought that this outburst would be temporary, but as the phenomenon lasted, as it grew more and more permanent, it became evident that this laughing matter, some called it a crisis, was here to stay and that humanity and animality had now entered the age of hilarity

drastic adjustments in social, political, economic, personal and international relations had to be made, thus U.S.P.E. was no longer a dream but instantly became a possible reality, a necessary reality which would put an end to all forms of kakistocracies

since the planet was now united in this spirit of gaiety, a mere formality was required to unify the world politically, the great laugh heard around the globe, as it would be called later, had transformed all political and social relations, and of course altered all human interactions, in a matter of a few months international and interpersonal transactions underwent major changes, the world was now full of smiling businessmen, jovial politicians and statesmen

this general gleefulness, however, not only transformed human attitudes toward the present, but also affected man's view of the past, consequently it was now possible to revise all previous interpretations of historical events, for if in the past it had been difficult, if not impossible, to take things seriously while

laughing or smiling, now everything was viewed and reviewed
with a smile, those who had maintained and were still maintain-
ing that it was impossible to think and smile at the same time
were being discredited with critical laughter, especially since it
was soon recognized that the simple act of smiling helps induce
a happy state of mind, or as the saying goes nowadays, Put on a
happy face for we are not just whistling misty

this theory of the happy face, formulated by the way in 1988,
five years before the international outburst of laughter, by
Professor Marrant, the old man's devoted friend who keeps
being mentioned here but who will not appear in person,
regrettably so, because he committed suicide in 1998, just
before he was to be deported to the space colonies, for his
number too had come up, but who was, at the time he formulated his controversial and quasi-prophetic theory, Director in
Chief of the Institute for the Study of Facial Expressions at the
University of Poznan, this theory of the happy face at any rate
explains several historical incongruities, for instance why Plato
argued that humor and laughter degrade art, religion, and
politics, and therefore should be avoided by civilized men, as
was indeed the case for centuries

perhaps Plato sensed that his deadpan utopia, Professor Marrant explained in his monograph, would never get off the
ground if the Philosopher Kings walked around sporting a big
grin on their faces, and even the Bible too frowns on laughter,
Marrant declared bluntly, substantiating this fact by quoting
from Ecclesiastes where it is written that Sorrow is better than
laughter for by the sadness of the countenance the heart is made
better, and even more interesting, Marrant went on to argue, is
the Bible's portrayal of a humorless Christ, therefore one can
rightly ask, as Marrant did, Did Jesus ever laugh, the New
Testament is mute on this point, it only states, explicitly
enough, that A fool lifteth up his voice in laughter but a wise
man doth scarce smile a little

it is understandable, therefore, why that still unexplained burst
of universal laughter, on April 13, 1993, on the very day when
the great Samuel Beckett celebrated his 87th birthday, if that

bit of information is of any consequence, caused such an uproar and transformed our world completely, and to a great extent was responsible for the creation of the new peaceful global society and the total revising of all human relations

in fact, when the space colonies were established, just a little over a year after this outburst, many people, young and old alike, were deported to these colonies because they refused or were unable to laugh or even smile a little, these nonlaughers and nonsmilers, as they are called, were found guilty of obstructing the shaping of the new hilarious society, as it is known today, however I should hasten to point out that this is not the case with our old man

quite the contrary, as Namredef and Moinous have confirmed in one of their recent reports, for they were told unequivocally, after having investigated this possibility with the appropriate authorities, that the old man had been rated quite high on the scale of human laughability, and in truth had always been regarded as a big-laugher, a happy-go-lucky smiler, even during the most critical moments of his life, the most adverse or humiliating situations, and in fact since that Friday in 1993, he has never forsaken his happy face, for as he explained himself on the solemn occasion of Professor Marrant's funeral which we all attended, If in the past, seriousness was looked upon as the dark backing that the mirror of life needed for us to understand anything, today it is clear, thanks to our departed friend's persistent optimism, that laughter is the translucent glass which allows us to perceive our survival

therefore once again we must seek some other reasons for our old man's expulsion, as Namredef and Moinous are still trying to do with all the necessary urgency, and that is why also I must continue to write this final report which began, you may recall, with the simple sentence, If the night passes quietly tomorrow, and so on

or let us say why I have undertaken this difficult task, quite unselfishly, for there is nothing in it for me, nothing, nor would I claim the presumptuousness of wanting to save humanity or

parts of it, no, certainly not, for as the old man once said to me
about himself, though I could say the same about myself, What
do I know of man's destiny, I could tell you more about radishes

though in my case it would have to be black rather than red
radishes, for I have an irrational passion for that clumsy ratlike
vegetable, but still I do believe that humanity can be improved
somewhat, and that is why, in spite of all the difficulties and
uncertainties ahead, I must persist in this project, and thus
perhaps prevent the deportation of my old man

VIII

It is 9:00 pm now, there is still hope, Namredef and Moinous have been gone a long time, something must be going on, they left hurriedly with the appropriate facial expression, the proper mask of gleefulness, compulsory these days, they had a thought, had it simultaneously

Do you think Moinous, that perhaps his association with

Merde alors, j'allais dire la même chose, Moinous cried out interrupting Namredef as though he had read his mind

a simultaneous bilingual thought

that, that perhaps his association with us may have had something to do with

Exactement

and they took off like two nervous stallions to explore this new possibility while I remain here rummaging through my notes, they must be at the spaceport by now

9:00 o'clock, there is still hope, three more hours before they cut him off from our life, yes there is still hope, especially when one remembers how, on December 22, 1849, the Tsar of Russia, Nicholas I, brimming with vanity commuted Dostoevsky's death sentence at the very moment when he faced the firing squad

true, Dostoevsky was deported to Siberia after that, how humiliating, but what the hell, he survived, he came back, came back to give us Crime and Punishment, The Idiot, The Possessed, and The Brothers Karamazov, that's better than nothing, no one has ever returned from the space colonies, no one so far, to my knowledge

but as long as there is time there is hope, or is it the reverse, three hours still before the departure, better get my ass going

remember the scene, how often it has been described to us, here let's go back and reread Leonid Grossman on the subject, I'm sure he won't mind if we refer to him a bit, hell it's part of the technique

There were twenty-one of them, condemned to death, they stood in front of a wooden platform covered with black cloth, Dostoevsky looked around, he recognized the orange walls of the guards' regimental barracks and the five golden cupolas of the massive cathedral, this was the square where the Semyonovsky regiment had its drills and parades, the condemned men were lined up at the rampart, there they were, thin, pale, unkempt, poets and jurists, engineers and officers, teachers and journalists, an entire Petrashevsky Friday, encircled by hand-picked troops in parade uniforms and mounted gendarmerie, with the military Governor-General of Petersburg, the Chief of Police, the Commanders of the Life Guards and the Tsar's chic aides-de-camp standing stiff and bored at their head, what a spectacle it must have been

the prisoners were led to the short staircase leading up to the platform and climbed the slippery steps while rifles darted upward with a precise clang and drums beat a nervous rat-tat-tat

Dostoevsky stumbled on the steps and almost fell, an old man behind him grabbed him by the arm, Careful Fyodor, this is not the time to break a leg, we still have a long way to go

Thank you old man, Dostoevsky said, as long as there is hope there is time

the final scene of the ritual had begun, an unbearable thought flashed through Dostoevsky's mind, What if I were not to die, what if my life were given back to me, what an eternity it would be

and then the auditor spoke, Having examined the case as presented by the army judiciary commission, the auditoriat-general finds all the accused guilty of planning to overthrow the state system and sentences them all to death by firing squad

So be it, His Majesty the Emperor of Russia had written in his own hand on the sentences

so be it, the accused had been dressed in loose gowns of coarse linen with pointed hoods attached and long sleeves that reached almost to the ground, suddenly the sound of lilting, insolent, prolonged laughter came from the scaffold, everyone turned to look, the heads of the soldiers swiveling on stiff shoulders like those of mechanical toys, Petrashevsky was shaking with uncontrollable laughter, Gentlemen, laughter was choking him, how ridiculous we must look in these clown's shirts

Dostoevsky was in the second row, next to the bearded old man who had helped him up the stairs, it could have been our old man, for all I know, or else his great-grandfather, after all we are extensions of the dead, they were both trying to look as contemptuous of authority as the rest of their comrades, Have courage old man, Dostoevsky whispered, look at them with scorn, I am, replied the old man, but like Dostoevsky he was listening to his heart beat

then the first three were called, Petrashevsky, Mombelli, Grigoryev, the three white ghosts descended from the platform, dragged their chained feet toward the wall of the rampart, Hoods down over the eyes, they were ordered, Petrashevsky shook the white hood off his face, threw his head backward, I am not afraid to look death in the eyes, he cried

the three were bound to gray posts with ropes, their arms pulled behind their backs and the long sleeves of the death shirts tied into a double knot, I have no more than a minute to live, Dostoevsky thought, his heart stood still in anticipation

Aim, the order came, the platoon took aim, it was a fearful moment indeed, the old man reached for Dostoevsky's hand, it was trembling, the terrible wait lasted for a full half minute, Why don't they fire, what's keeping them, the rifles were still pointing at the three prisoners as if toying with them

one of the Tsar's aides-de-camp was galloping across the parade ground, the sound of the horse's hooves on the cobblestones ringing the final death knell

all this of course had been carefully rehearsed, staged for the perfect melodramatic effect, the death sentences had already been commuted four days earlier, but the accused didn't know that

Let the swines suffer the agony of death to the last possible moment, the Tsar was rubbing his gloved hands together and pacing the floor angrily when he spoke these words, four days earlier in his palace, Yes let them face their death and then give them life again, humiliate them with life in a grandiose gesture of magnanimity

and now General Sumarokov read from the sealed packet the aide-de-camp had just handed him, Retired Engineer-Lieutenant Fyodor Dostoevsky, having read the report submitted to Him with loyal feelings, His Majesty generously commutes your death sentence and orders your deportation to penal servitude in fortresses for four years, and after that four more years of military service as a common soldier in the Emperor's Caucasian Corps the General read each commutation, twenty-one of them, in a resounding dispassionate tone of voice, I'm skipping details here

the prisoners did not speak, did not let out cries of joy or sighs of relief, no, they stood calm, contemptuous, and scornful

By His Majesty's order the convict Butashevich-Petrashevsky shall set out for Siberia directly from the execution site accompanied by a gendarme and a courier

I wish to take leave of my comrades, Petrashevsky said to the Commandant, and swaying in his chains he dragged his fettered feet clumsily from one man to the next, kissed each one and bade him farewell, then he faced his companions, Do not lose heart, my friends, let them put us in irons, these chains are a priceless bracelet fashioned for us by the wisdom of the West and the spirit of the age which penetrates everywhere, and placed on us by our love of mankind, two guards pulled him away

Dostoevsky had tears in his eyes, What an unbearable eternity, he thought, then as the prisoners were led away from the scaffold he said to the old man, Do not despair old man, certainly we shall all rise again, certainly we shall see each other and shall tell each other with joy and gladness all that has happened

with these prophetic words Dostoevsky unknowingly had already spoken the end of The Brothers Karamazov, and so the old man replied while embracing Dostoevsky, Ah, how splendid it will be

later that day, back in his cell after the ordeal of this mock execution, awaiting the moment of his deportation, Dostoevsky wrote a letter to his brother Mikhail, I'm quoting here from this immortal document

My brother, I do not feel despondent and have not lost heart, life is life everywhere, life is in ourselves and not outside us, there will be men beside me, and the important thing is to be a man among men and to remain a man always, whatever the misfortunes, not to despair and not to fall, that is the aim of life, that is its purpose, I realize this now, the idea has entered into my flesh and my blood, yes that is the truth, that head which created, which lived the higher life of art, which experienced and had grown accustomed to the necessities of the spirit, that head has already been severed from my shoulders, what remains is memory and images, those I created and those I have not yet given form to, true, they will corrode me, but I have still got my heart and the same flesh and blood which can love and suffer and pity and remember, and that is also life, never before have I felt such abundant and healthy reserves of spiritual life in me as now, never before

that letter, full of optimism and unshakable faith in his vocation and his future renascence, could have been written by our old man, yes that letter, or one very much like it, might still be written by our old man before midnight, on this sad new year's eve 1999

or perhaps, at this very moment, as he sits in that antechamber of departure, he is speaking the same words, or words like those of Dostoevsky to my faithful co-workers who must be standing next to him in awkward grief, and who will report these words to me later when they return

but that's Dostoevsky's story, and he survived, our old man's story is something else, just as sad, yes, just as gruesome, perhaps even more, for he too missed an appointment with death, without knowing it, oh so long ago, that day in 1942, when he stood in one of the communal shower rooms of Auschwitz with some fifty others like him, humiliated by their nakedness, fifty rickety pale bluish bodies already half into moribundity, that day when they all stood looking alike, familiar and familial, each old man in that group resembling his father, and each old woman resembling his mother, was it an hallucination, and the others too, the younger ones, all of them looking like him, like his sisters and the brothers he never had, fifty depersonalized replicas of himself standing in shame, covering their sex with their hands, shivering in the cold on that exceptional day when, against the very rules of the camp, men and women were pushed into the shower room together, as a mocking coed spectacle, and waited for the water to spill on their bodies, or whatever came out of those shower heads to cleanse the dreckigen Juden

but that day, for some unknown reason, the water did not flow on these bluish bodies, nothing happened, did the camp commandant, or perhaps the Führer himself, in a wild stroke of generosity, commute the death sentences for that day, as a playful gesture, for the fun of it, or was the water frozen in the pipes, the gas solidified, but unlike the mock execution of Dostoevsky and his friends, it was never revealed whether there had been a commutation or not, or if the whole scene had been cynically prearranged, staged, rehearsed for perfect melodramatic effect

as the Jews were led back to their barracks, walking naked in the snow, the old man also composed a letter in his mind, a message which, of course, he never had a chance to put on paper, and therefore never sent to anyone, but it began this way, Something happened today, I do not know what it is, an end, or perhaps a beginning, I do not feel discouraged, broken, just confused, debased, what is certain is that there are no principles in this world, only events, no laws, only circumstances, how ridiculous we must have looked in our naked expectancy

and later, his death now behind him, his death temporarily postponed, perhaps even cancelled, he wondered, Did it happen to me or have I imagined the whole thing, something happened to somebody, yes to others, millions of others, to my father, to my mother, my sisters, to all of them, but not to me, no not to me, that ultimate moment of degradation, the unspeakable event

during the night, after he folded his tattooed wrist under his head, he dreamed, and in his dream a giant hoof struck his double face as he saw himself kneel before himself to suck the blood from his mythical flesh where dirty nails had scratched away the remains of an unspeakable numerical name, erased the fragments of his story, and cut an ugly wound into the pigments of his race

and so that day, in 1942, he too like Dostoevsky was humiliated with an excess of life, he too suffered the insult of survival, and yet he could not tell if it had really happened to him

years later, whenever the old man remembered that scene, or replayed it in his mind, as every human being, every adult must have replayed that scene at least once in his life, must have imagined how it felt to be standing in that gas chamber, yes once, whether or not one had been there, he would hear the words of Maimonides echo in his head, Every Jew is like an actor playing a Jew, each gives his own interpretation of the past, and indeed the old man understood then that one must always live from a sense that the end, the Apocalypse has already happened, a sense that nothing has yet begun, that man has not yet been created, that everything is on the verge of starting again, yes each time he replayed that ugly scene in his mind he understood that it was now possible to start anew, every day, and to confirm this notion one of his friends, his name escapes me now, once told him how, in this spirit of perpetual new beginnings, he had written a story which opens with a writer who, in order to get started, shoots himself, his blood hits the wall and spells out this message, It is important to begin when everything is already over

in a way this postponement of the end, this transition from lessness to endlessness, this shift from ultimate to penultimate or even to antepenultimate, seems to adumbrate a greater mystery, a greater horror too, and that is why perhaps our old man must be expelled from this world, one cannot wander forever in a borrowed land, live a deferred life, but of course I am only speculating here

perhaps nothing happened that day, it was not like that, how do I know, I wasn't there, no I was lucky, indeed I have never been and hopefully will never be deported, let's just say that I was fortunate, though I could easily be in the old man's place now, and he in mine in this room writing my story

that would greatly facilitate matters, for I already know, or let's say I have a notion of how this story might end, Moinous and Namredef would come to see me in my antechamber of departure where I would be sitting resigned, the buzzing of my past in my ears, a faithful old dog crouched next to me like a sphinx, and they would ask, with the necessary tone of urgency, Why are you being sent to the colonies

and me, at the last moment, just as the huge metallic doors would slide open and reveal the impatient giant spaceship pointing skyward on the launching pad, I would tell them quietly, There are no such things as the space colonies

What, they would cry out totally mystified, you mean to say

Yes of course, it's not true, maybe in the future there will be such places, but for the time being it's not possible, I mean technologically, it's a lie, a myth, I have invented the space colonies so that I can be sent there, imaginatively speaking

But why, why

To get rid of the burden of my past, you might say

But then, they would ask disconcerted, what do they do with all the people, all those poor devils who are sent, who have been sent to those colonies for years now, since 1994 in fact, and what about these people here, today, including yourself

Oh that's not a lie, that's a fact, a reality, they are dumped into space, into the vast expanse of receding space, like human garbage, detritus, and the bodies float, they float away into gaslessness

wow, that would make a striking ending, a bit too sad perhaps, and too melodramatic, but what an ending, all those bodies floating in space toward the edges of the universe, millions and millions of decomposed bodies speeding backward into the great cunt of space, inside the original black hole of the Big Bang, millions of bodies twinkling like tiny yellow stars

except that it won't work, the situation is otherwise, in reality I am sitting here writing this story, or contemplating how it will be written eventually, while the old man waits in the antechamber of departure, and we still don't know why he is there

of course one can speculate, as we have been doing now for quite some time, and indeed what can one do but speculate, speculate, until one hits on the happy speculation, When all goes silent, and comes to an end, it will be because the words have been said, those it behoved to say, no need to know which, no means of knowing which, they'll be there somewhere, in the heap, in the torrent, not necessarily the last, they have to be ratified by the proper authority, that takes time, damn right, Sam would say, but what better way to pass the time

perhaps my old man himself has also imagined the space colonies in order to be virtually deported there, invented them in spite of me, and in spite of Moinous and Namredef, to get rid of the guilt of having survived the Holocaust, I wouldn't put it past him

after all does it really matter if one was there or not, does it really matter in the long run if one experienced the gas chambers or if one merely imagines how it must have been, the Holocaust was a universal affair, a total affair in which all mankind was implicated and is still implicated, therefore to speak of that sad affair, in life or in fiction, in an effort to come to terms with its incomprehensibility, must also be a collective undertaking, and of course the same can be said of the space colonies, real or imagined, it doesn't make much difference if it is he or I in that antechamber of departure, after a while we all become interchangeable

we are all displaced persons surviving in a strange land, in life as well as in fiction, and so why not ask, even if it is in vain, as it is asked in The Book of Questions, Old man tell us the story of your country, and speaking for all of us he would answer, as Yukel does, I have no country, I am an old man, and my life is the story

in my case, however, were I in his place, I suppose I would have to answer, making a crucial inversion of the terms, The story is my life, me there, me here, what's the difference, me now, me then, comes out the same in the end, I could have been this man, we share the same solitude

yes, we have walked in the same shadow, even though I am only a middleman in this undertaking, but unfortunately the potential readers of this story may jump to the conclusion, false and hasty as it may be, that this story is autobiographical in the sense that it tells in a sort of camouflaged way the life of the author, namely me disguised as a nameless old man, projected into a fictitious future space, as in fact one such reader has already suggested upon seeing what has been told so far of the old man's story, but this is not true, I assure you, for if it were so then indeed I would be the one sitting in that antechamber of departure, remembering how I imagined the space colonies in order to be deported there, while the old man, or someone like him, would be here in this room writing me, inventing and twisting my life into premembrances, distorting my self, my many selves into a strange time loop

why pretend otherwise, and were this to be so then there would definitely be something wrong with the twofold vibration theory which sustains this extemporaneous story

for as we all know, just as the child says his first name to speak of himself, the writer names himself through an infinity of fictitious third persons, it's the norm, even though it doesn't mean a damn thing, contained in me now are all my previous and potential selves, it's inevitable, and the same of course goes for our old man, but why should this suggest that I am camouflaging my life, my past, in this story, what good would that do the writer merely turns experience into words, he displaces, symbolizes, simulates, dissimulates, reinvents, but it's always a betrayal of the original experience, a flagrant falsification, that's how it goes in the Funhouse of fiction, a simple matter of piling up words, words, and more words, that's what my old man's life is all about

of course all this is pure speculation, a necessary digression to pass the time while Moinous and Namredef are out there, urgently investigating the situation, and perhaps they will return soon with the truth, the real story, the final word, and we shall know once and for all if the old man can be saved, but meanwhile that gives me time to put some order here, clean my typewriter, change the ribbon, cut my nails, consult my notes, eat a sandwich, take a nap even

they must be at the spaceport by now

IX

It's all over

Moinous and Namredef come rushing into my study, It's all over, they cry out in unison, they are out of breath, flustered and disheveled, with sweat dripping down from their foreheads, even though it is the middle of winter, and darn cold on this new year's night, way past midnight now, from the disconcerted expression on their faces, I cannot tell if they are relieved or horrified, It's all over, they keep repeating

That's it, it's finished, I utter anticipating the worse

No wait, wait a minute, give us a chance to catch our breath, we'll explain the whole thing, from the beginning, from the moment we got there, hold your horses

Come on you guys, tell me dammit, tell me what happened, you can't keep me in suspense like this, it's not fair, we've already entered the new year, the new century

they calm down, Moinous is wiping his brow with a large colored handkerchief while Namredef, who has removed his tweed jacket, unbuttons his vest to breathe more easily, Do you have anything to drink, they ask as they both settle down on the sofa

I pour them a generous glass of Calvados from the bottle I keep in the drawer of my desk, I prefer it to Cognac, Here, but drink slowly, I say as I sit backward on a chair, facing them, notebook in hand, go ahead, I'm listening

We arrived at the spaceport, must have been around 9:30, we arrived at the spaceport, the place was in a state of feverish activity, must have been just about 9:30, teeming with people, and

Hey hold on, one at the time, please, I'm getting all confused, how do you expect me to take notes if you guys speak together

Okay, you go ahead Nam, you tell him what happened

No, you do it Moimoi

Come on you guys, let's not play games here, skip the decorum and let's get on with it

Namredef begins again, We arrived at the spaceport, must have been around 9:30, and were led immediately to his antechamber of departure by one of the attendants, no problems so far, thousands of other visitors were there too, spending these last few hours like us, I suppose, with relatives, friends, acquaintances who were on the list of deportees, the place was bustling with activity, one could feel the tension, though hardly perceptible, yes everything seemed normal, no shouting, no crying, no twisting of hands, isn't that right Moinous

Yes just like any other day, we expected something else, you know what I mean, more excitement, Moinous explains while swallowing a mouthful of Calvados, more anxiety, both from the visitors and the deportees, after all this was the ultimate moment, so to speak, on the contrary there was even a feeling of festivity in the air, true, it was new year's eve, we even heard faint laughter coming from the other antechambers, it was strange, people seemed to be enjoying this moment, there was no great panic

Hopelessness sometimes gets more laughs than hope, I say to let them know that I understand what they are talking about, But get to the point, what about the old man

Well, when we came in we found him, as we had on the other occasions of our past visits, still sitting on his trunk, head between his hands, an almost classical pose by now, staring blankly in front of him, faithful old Sam asleep close to his feet folded into a black and white polka dot ball, perfect picture of quiet resignation

Can you skip the fucking lyrical details, I say somewhat anxious to hear the rest of the story

I don't think he was aware of how little time there was left, Namredef continues ignoring my impatience, and as soon as we walked in, without even greeting us or reacting to our obvious concerned looks, he started talking, raving rather, yes he did sound a bit delirious, he didn't really address us directly, no it was as if he was pursuing a dialogue with someone who had been there before we came

The peculiar character of human reality, he was saying, is that it is without excuse, as Freud once said, nothing is gratuitous except death, everybody eventually learns this, yes life is not necessary, it is contingent

Oh shit, I whispered to Moinous, he is in one of his moods, I doubt we'll get anything out of him, at this point we were still hoping that he might reveal to us the reason for his being here, I mean for being on the list of deportees for that night, and that we might still, in spite of the short time left, be able to prevent his departure, you know, register a final protest with the authorities, after all wasn't that what you told us to do, Get something out of him, he must know the reason

How are you, we asked to start the conversation, to get something going

Fine, fine, he replied absently, but went on with his monologue, there is a frightening implication in our predicament that through all eternity there will always remain some sliver of life, some thin slice of humanity simmering helplessly in the great casserole of the universe, he smiled, yes it is impossible to erase consciousness completely from human nature, remarkable fact which not only justifies the organic interpretation of the human phenomenon, but also opens the way to solid anticipation concerning our future destiny and even the fate reserved to us at the end of time, out there in the Noosphere, lost in that immense unthinking machine of the universe

Didn't you try to point out to him the urgency of the moment, I ask, I mean why didn't you

Of course we tried, but he ignored us, I don't know, he seemed absent from his own presence, and we too, in that room, began to feel absented from ourselves, it's hard to explain, it was as though a veil had been pulled over our eyes, and we were being pushed inside ourselves to find there a dark chamber, you know, like that of a camera, a dark zone of indifference where the accidents of nature, I suppose that's the only thing one can call them, were reproduced under a distorted form which made them ungraspable, the old man seemed to be slipping away from us, that's how it felt

Yes that's exactly how it felt, Moinous amplifies, we didn't seem to be able to relate to him, suddenly there was an unbridgeable gap between us, and nothing seemed to matter any more

after a moment of silence he started ranting again, Oh earth, you old extinguisher, will I ever again feel your sweet durability, he was stamping the plastic floor under his feet as he said that, stamping it with a cheerlessness beyond sarcasm, he paused, Ah well, can't complain, no no, mustn't complain, so much to be grateful for

What the hell could we say to that, Namredef shrugs his shoulders, he sounded like old Winnie sinking into her mound of earth, you know in Happy Days, casually observing her own burial

He's always been full of literary junk, I remark while scribbling a note to remind myself to check the page reference, just in case, yes always full of classics, but what good did it do him

Forced to live incessantly within myself, he went on, for the last ten years or so, in fact since the Dismarital Law of 1990 was passed, and not sharing with anyone the sweet but secret joys of my mental activity, he hesitated, well joys or pains

What do you mean, we interrupted, we were there with you most of the time, you could have shared with us

Yes I know my friends, you were there, but still it was as though I was seeking to resolve the work of my destiny through evasion, and I remained in this almost vegetal state like—he searched for the right word, like an anchorite, he finally said without a trace of a smile on his face, yes an anchorite

You, an anchorite, of all people, come on you're kidding yourself, we said with a chuckle in our voices in an effort to break through the opacity of his discourse, That's bordering on self-indulgence, but he didn't pay attention to our objection, he went on, though now he seemed to be speaking more directly to us, and with more intensity

As you know, I've always preferred action to thinking, movement to contemplation, but suddenly it seemed that I had reversed the very principle that had governed my life, I no longer acted, no longer produced, no more words came out of me, I mean coherent words, from the simple fact of thinking to the exterior fact of rendering thoughts into words, there was something which destroyed my mental process, something which prevented me from being what I wanted to be, and which left me, how shall I say, in suspense

That's not unusual with people like us, we mumbled for lack of anything better to say

he ignored that remark, I had become cataleptic, a scary condition to be in for a man like me, only once in a while fragments, pieces of language would burst out but which seemed totally meaningless and useless to me, you know fractured sentences that could not be connected, things like, Bird into head flew, or this one, Voice never apprehended entirely echoes space of future, yes fragments like these, Bird in retrospect for remade self caught in unself present, Region of ruins full circle into fingers back to voice, I remember these pieces so clearly, they still haunt me, but what the hell can you do with crap like that

we didn't say anything, it was all so vague, and yet we could feel how desperate he was to tell us about those difficult years, but what was the use at this late stage

he continued, My mental life had become a whirlpool, a cesspool of verbal mush, and more and more I was acting like a cephalopod

You understand, Moinous and Namredef explain to me apologetically, that we couldn't make much sense of what he was talking about, it all sounded so evasive to us

Perhaps he was giving you guys a clue, the clue to his present predicament, but you missed the point

No, we thought of that, we even discussed it, the two of us, when for a few moments he dozed off, right there, still sitting on his metallic box, in the middle of a sentence, he even snored a little

Sounds like a confession, Moinous said to me

But so unlike him, I replied, have you ever heard him confess anything in his life, and yet it occurred to us that perhaps he was giving us the reason for his being here, that he was in fact telling us, indirectly, in that twisted manner of his, why he was among the deportees, that he was at last admitting his uselessness

But somehow that didn't seem right, Moinous cuts in, no, we even talked about the possibility that the fact he had not produced anything in the last ten years, even though like everyone else we were under the impression that he was working on something important, had rendered him useless to himself and to society, and consequently, you know what I mean, the usual patati patata, but how could a man of such vitality, a man of raw energy like him fall into such a state of complete inactivity, it didn't make sense, especially since we were always there with him, we would have noticed it, unless of course he was pretending, but even so, how can you pretend to be active, how can you hide inactivity by pretending to be active, it's absurd, it cannot be done, it's a contradiction in itself, either you do something or you don't, but you cannot do to do nothing

Yes I agree, it does seem paradoxical, though you know there have been many such cases lately, cases of people pretending to live an active life whereas in fact they secretly wallow in lethargy, and this to keep up with the maddening rythm of our time, out of fear of old age

It's true, Namredef shakes his head affirmatively, but not our old man, he was always ahead of his time, as you know, always three steps in front of everyone else, and when it comes to old age, he made a mockery of it, don't you remember, even two years ago he was still screwing a young chick like he was twenty years old, remember that gorgeous creature he met in Texas, they were wild together, what a sweet thing she was, and up to a few months ago that old geezer was still playing a mean game of tennis, blowing everybody off the courts

Nam is right, Moinous says, but still, when he awoke after that little nap, we asked him, Do you think that perhaps it is because of this unproductiveness of yours that your number came up

Oh no, no, absolutely not, no one suspected anything, quite the contrary, everyone was under the impression, as you were yourselves dear friends, that I was working on something important, that I was in the process of deducing an entirely new epistemological system from the fragments of my thoughts, whatever that means

Yes indeed, it seemed so, but what happened then

My restless history, my voracious dreams deserted me, everything fell apart, I became silent, memoryless, it was as though I was waiting on the edge of an abyss, waiting for a future and ready to let the first sensitive being I met invent one for me, push me over that precipice, but no one came along

What about that beautiful girl from Texas, Moinous asked, wasn't she sensitive enough

Oh she was sensitive and beautiful, and so kind to me, but that's not what I mean, I'm talking metaphorically, but in any event, one day I realized that I had no more ideas, no ideas as such, that I was totally devoid of ideas, empty, still I thought I might be able to go on, make of this emptiness an occasion, because, I told myself, the basic principle of communication itself, that is to say how to translate the facts, the immediate sensations of experience into an alternative structure of language, constitutes an idea in itself, an idea about not having ideas, and I saw in this a possibility of survival, after all integrity in art is more complicated than being rich or poor, famous or not, austere in purpose or advanced in ideas, it's always a question of personal survival, that's what I told myself

Yes, sounds interesting, so what did you do, I asked while Moinous was mumbling to himself, Personally I could have survived forever with that gorgeous Texas girl, she was some dish

Nothing, nothing at all, because even to achieve such a project one needs words, and words were lacking, I began to suffer fits of discouragement which coincided with the moment when I ceased to believe in words, or when words ceased to serve me, when I felt words were failing me, evading me, oh I managed to fake it for a while, made believe that I was still working, but it was a lie, and gradually I withdrew into the hollow of my mind, cut myself off from the rest of the world

He's always been extremely lucid about his work and about his own shortcomings, I say as I light a cigarette, a true intellectual who refused to develop the kind of protective blindness most artists use to shield their art from an excess of knowledge, yes it always amazed me how tough and uncompromising he was with himself and with his work, but what did you say to him after that

All this is very revealing, we said, we had no idea you were going through such difficult times, if only you had told us, but still, we continued, what does all this have to do with your being here

Nothing, nothing I know of, he replied calmly, I didn't say it had anything to do with it, I'm simply answering your questions, or perhaps I am closing the books on myself, then he stopped talking, got up and started pacing back and forth in the narrow antechamber, not even paying attention to us any longer, as if we had already departed, meanwhile Sam opened one droopy eye to follow his master, but without lifting his lazy head which was resting on his paws, we suddenly felt as though we were in excess in that room

All this is indeed revealing, I say to Moinous and Namredef as I pour them and myself another glass of Calvados, yes me too for years I had noticed how reluctant he had become to speak, or rather how incoherent and evasive his language had become

Yes, exactly, we sensed with what difficulty words were rising in that tall body that kept accusing itself of behaving like a scarecrow, but since he was going on, we didn't question him, we only wondered, where do they come from these words that refuse to be spoken, hesitate to be articulated, from some obscure zone inside of him where they take shape hesitantly, if not painfully, and more and more they were brief, curt, cutting, nasal, pitiless, and yet we could sense how they would have liked so much to be generous, those words, or even just affable, somehow we felt grateful to him for waiting, for waiting interminably while the words struggled so hard to detach themselves from his flesh

That's a very nice way to put it, Namredef says to Moinous, and yet we didn't do a damn thing to help him, standing in that room like two dejected clowns who have messed up their act, while he kept walking back and forth, dragging his feet along the ground, we stood awkwardly in a corner and felt sorry for ourselves, and as we watched him it became clear to us how his recent gloominess, his long silences, his lassitude had affected us, it seemed that after each visit with him we returned full of contradictory ideas, more and more confused

You don't have to tell me that, it was obvious that the two of you were no longer in control of the situation

What did you expect, Moinous and Namredef cry out, it was unnerving, the sight of our old friend sitting in that room, especially these last few weeks, exercised on us a sinister influence, and we feared to find ourselves caught in this mood where lassitude becomes contagious, in a way we were affected by his condition

Maybe you did catch whatever he was suffering from, I say, but you know the old man's successes or failures are really a matter of interpretation, I hesitate to say this, but perhaps you are the ones who failed to report correctly the exactitude of his predicament and of his mental state, after all you were my sole contact with him

Well I'll be damned, what are you trying to do, shove the guilt on us, blame us for the deficiencies of your own work

Not at all, what I am doing I am doing for him who matters a great deal to me, as you know, and not for myself, of whom I constantly despair, but as the secondhand teller of this story, what do I know, what is my knowledge, just an artifact, an object created by skill, by cunning, arts plus factum, interpretation built upon what has presumably been perceived and reported by you, but not corresponding exactly with the empiricities of your primary observations, your original reactions, that's inevitable in such matters

Oh I see, Moinous says throwing his arms up in the air in disgust, now you're saying that we are the ones who failed in this undertaking while you sat here, cozy like a monk, fiddling with your notes and your typewriter, and we did all the work, all the dirty work, and got the lousy runaround from everybody, well that's gratitude for you

No, that's not it, you don't see what I mean, in this intramural presentation of ours the author's vision can only be as sharp and bright, or as blind and perverted, as that of the narrators, the two of you, after all, and I should have perhaps mentioned it earlier for the good of our potential readers, you are half blind Moinous, it's been noticeable all along, no use denying it, and as for you my dear Namredef, we all know that you are hard of hearing, a birth defect, nothing we can do about that, it's unfortunate, but it does draw a veil of uncertainty on what you two guys see and hear, and what you report

Now he says it, don't you think it's a little late to make that kind of revelation, what are you trying to do, discredit us

All right, you'll tell me that I should have done something about that sooner, or at least allowed for some discrepancy in your reports, all I can tell you is that I had no one else to turn to, but what has been clear to me from the beginning, more or less, is that your words as narrators have constantly focused our gaze on their own considerations about the old man's predicament, however doubtful these considerations may have been, and therefore they, and they alone could save him, I agree it was clever of me to have transferred the narrative responsibility to you, but what else could I do, it was the only way I could proceed with this story, I had no other choice, or let's say that all other choices were abandoned

Clever he says, it was a sneaky, dirty, dishonest little trick, what a hypocrite you are

Nonetheless, I say pretending not to notice their gestures of outrage, that is why you two could never speak dogmatically, how could you, but only with uncertainty, our story could not function any other way, because you see what counts in this final report is not so much what you have thought of this or that, what you have or have not seen or heard, but what immediately systematizes you within the sequence of events, or if you prefer what fictionalizes you

Now he tells us, what a bastard you are, according to you then we're just two broken-down puppets who have no will of our own, in fact it's not even sure if we exist

No, let me explain, and stop distorting what I'm saying, the effects of life are visible, but life itself is not, it cannot be, especially in our kind of extemporaneous situation, in the last resort it is action, function, movement, improvisation, that which cannot be totally seen, drawn, grasped, described in its plenitude, that counts, the rest is imposture, mere speculation

Here he goes again with his speculative crap, they both cry out, this time truly exasperated, where does that leave us

You don't get it, in the case of our old man as with all historical events, at first it was a matter of observing and classifying, then it became a matter of rationalizing and explaining, we failed in both instances, and now, at the stage where we are, desperate as we are of ever being able to assert the facts, it's a matter of imagining and projecting, that's the only thing we can do, the only hope left

All this is well and good, but it doesn't resolve a damn thing for us in the immediate present, what do we do now, I mean right now, at this very moment, Namredef asks

What do you mean what do we do now, it's obvious, we go on with this report, as best we can, you tell me what happened next at the spaceport, how long the old man went on talking, pacing back and forth in that room, and so on

Well all right, if you think it'll help, Namredef says as he sits down again on the sofa next to Moinous, facing me, and continues to relate what happened at the spaceport

By then the two of us were getting annoyed with the old man's evasiveness, his total disregard for our presence, Goddammit, we finally shouted at him, why don't you come out with it, tell us, once and for all, tell us why you are in this fucking place, give us the facts

There are no facts, he answered calmly, his mouth twisted into a disarming smile, no facts to be accurately described, only hypotheses to be set up, no choices of words will express the truth, for one has only a choice of rhetorical masks in a situation like this one

That's all he said, I ask feeling myself losing patience, didn't he show some anguish at least

None, he just went on for a long time, but not saying anything, I mean anything that made sense to us, and yet we were captivated by the flow of words which came out of him, he even told us some stories, some of the old stories, you know the one about the little boy in the closet, the one about the raw potatoes on the train, the one about the noodles, Ah le temps des nouilles, he said laughing, and the story about the farm, and the lampshade factory, and that funny one about his 1947 Buick-special that landed in a tree during a snowstorm, the same old stories he'd told us so many times over the years, he went on for a long time, once in a while breaking into laughter in the middle of his own stories, and we did too, totally engrossed, unaware of the time and of the place where we were, he's always been a captivating storyteller, in fact we had lost track of the time when suddenly an announcement came over the loudspeakers

in the ceiling of the room, must have been around eleven o'clock
or so

You've never mentioned there were loudspeakers in the ceiling

We hadn't noticed them before, a kind of intercom system, I
suppose that's how they communicate with the deportees, in
any event a voice said, We are now entering the final phase of
our operation, will all travelers proceed immediately to the hall
of departure, visitors may accompany the travelers to that hall
but must not, I repeat, must not advance beyond the railings
that delimit the area marked for visitors, attendants will direct
traffic and answer questions, further instructions will be given
in the hall of departure

Moinous and I panicked, but the old man seemed calm, almost
relieved, Let's go, he said without any show of emotion, he
even insisted on carrying the trunk himself, No at least let us
carry it for you, we said somewhat embarrassed with our own
pleading words, it's heavy, but he wouldn't let us, To each his
little box, he said jokingly as he hoisted the trunk on his
shoulder, almost effortlessly, that old man of ours was really in
great shape, and we started down the long cold metallic corridors, it was a long walk to the waiting hall, red arrows indicated
the direction, from the other antechambers travelers and their
visitors were also proceeding quietly

Hey, what about the dog, I ask

Oh, the dog, I almost forgot, just as we were ready to leave the
antechamber, two attendants in blue coveralls came in, one of
them had a leash, you know the kind that slips over the animal's
head into a choker, without saying a word he put it around
Sam's neck, the old dog sensed that something was going on
and started pulling away but without barking, just whining as if
he had been wounded, he tried to plant his claws into the floor
but it was so slippery, so hard, that plastic floor, he was sliding
along as the attendants pulled him toward the door, the old man
bent down to pat the dog on the rump and Sam looked up at

him imploringly with those droopy bloodshot eyes of his, the old man turned his head away, and you won't believe this, suddenly he kicked the dog in the ribs, oh not hard, no, but just enough for poor Sam to groan, and then the dog quietly followed the attendants out into the corridor

So what happened after that

You mean to Sam

No to the old man

Oh let me tell him the rest, Moinous pleads, I think I got all the details

Okay, you take over Moimoi, I have to go to the john anyway, Namredef says as he walks to the bathroom door

Shall I wait for you, Moinous asks

No go ahead, I'll only be a minute

Moinous clears his throat, As soon as we entered the hall of departure we were separated from the old man, it was so quick, no time even to shake hands with him, or anything like that, we stood behind the railings where thousands of visitors were already crowded, and more were pouring in, we were way in the back, the old man was led to the lines of deportees, but he was so tall, and his head so large that we could see him from where we stood, on tiptoe, everything was extremely well organized, and for reasons undoubtedly opposed to sentimental harmony, the deportees were facing the enormous steel doors which were open, of course, and one could see the huge sleek spaceship on the launching pad, it was all gray, dozens of attendants, some in blue others in red coveralls, some on foot and others driving little electric carts that beeped and hummed and whizzed around, made sure that everyone went to the right place, they barked orders through megaphones, they had to because the place was quite noisy by now, it reminded me of the old days in busy train stations, you know the hubbub, the excitement, the anticipation of going somewhere, yes it was very much like that, like the old train stations

Jesus, have you ever seen so many people in one place, I shouted to Namredef above the pell-mell babel from the vast crowd of mixed people, I mean people of all nationalities, races, colors, sizes and shapes, young and old, and lots of children too, on both sides of the railings, with the visitors and among the deportees, and all these people, packed together like sardines, herded together like cattle, or whatever other metaphor you might think appropriate, were jostling each other, pushing and shoving to get a better look, and was it cold in that place, you could see the cold air, the fog coming out of people's mouths like cigarette smoke as they breathed, lucky we had on our heavy winter overcoats, but not the old man, like all the other travelers he was wearing the traditional white tunic of the deportees that fell all the way down to his ankles

both Namredef and I were crushed by the sheer enormity of the hall which was lit by bright yellow disks in the ceiling, the entire room, even the floor and ceiling, was made of shiny gray metal and, except for the huge doors opened to the spaceship positioned just outside the hall, there was not a single seam in the structure, yes it's true, not a single seam anywhere, ask Namredef, we both noticed it, which meant that when the giant doors were shut the hall was totally airproof, waterproof, and presumably soundproof as well, I tell you the place was so gigantic, so incredibly big that twenty-five Arcs de Triomphe could easily fit inside that great hall of departure, Namredef argued with me that the right number was more like thirty, but I told him it was the wrong moment to start such a petty argument, twenty-five or thirty, what's the big difference, I told him, there is a point where even numbers become meaningless, but that gives you an idea of the incredible size of this place, we stood there mouths open, gazing up and around, oppressed by the vastness of this hall, feeling quite insignificant, like tiny blemishes in this seamless bubble of metal perfection

Yes, we were overwhelmed, Namredef cuts in as he picks up

the narrative, crushed, but then I asked Moinous, Where the hell did the old man go, I can't see him anywhere, somehow while looking at the place we had lost sight of him

He's right over there, in the middle of the second group, in front of the ship, I yelled back pointing since it wasn't too hard to spot the old man, even at such a great distance he stood out towering above the others, and though the travelers looked alike in their white tunics he was unmistakable in that anonymous group, they were all facing away from us toward the gaping doors, but that tall figure out there became our sole concern, our north star, you might say, as we were desperately trying to work our way closer to the railings, but the crowd was so tightly pressed together that it was difficult to move either forward or backward, yet somehow with great efforts, by pushing our elbows into people's sides, who were of course doing the same to us, we managed to gain a few paces, the old man was now more clearly visible from where we stood, especially against the background of the silvery spaceship framed by the open doors and nearly as tall, it was like a double exposure, I mean the old man and the spaceship standing there superimposed, except that this giant cylinder with its tapered nosecone and its two spherical fuel tanks attached on each side looked like a poised prick in erection pulsating in the cloudless black sky, ready to gather within itself those yellowish spermatoid-like bodies and then penetrate the great cunt of space

Attention, Attention, blared the two thirty-six-foot loudspeakers mounted high on the walls on each side of the doors, the voice echoed thunderously for several seconds as the crowd became hushed, All departees will report immediately to the embarkation platform outside when their name is called, boomed the voice through the hall, Visitors will not be allowed to loiter in the waiting area after the person with whom they are associated has departed, visitors must leave the hall instantly

a tremor circulated through the crowd, Namredef grabbed my arm and squeezed it hard, This is it, he said

Sarah Bialek, called out the loudspeakers after a brief pause, the name was repeated a second time, Sarah Bialek, then Michel Deguy, Joseph Francavilla, Shigeo Hamano, Zoltan Abadi-Nagy, Larry McCaffery, David Porush, Ihab Hassan, Mas'ud Zavarzadeh, each name repeated twice, we were listening intently, not only trying to hear when the name of the old man would be called but to determine the nationality or ethnic origin of the deportees according to their names, mere curiosity on our part, and also trying to recognize if perchance some of the names were familiar to us, Erica Hubscher, Robin Murez, Jacques Ehrmann, David Naimark, Ernest Blake, Richard Martin, Joseph Toungaian, Loulou Jacobson, Ramon Hombre della Pluma, Suce Mapomme, and so on, one after the other, as the voice droned through the long list of names and the deportees moved forward, each carrying his or her metal trunk

at first we thought the names were being called alphabetically, but it soon became obvious to us that they were called at random, or according to some order which we could not determine, we could see each person, as his or her name was called and called again, being motioned forward by the attendants and led quickly toward the spaceship, without any resistance, and at the same time, almost simultaneously, the visitors for that person would leave the waiting area, calmly and docilely, it was a slow process, but relentless and uninterrupted, and gradually the crowd around us diminished as the lines of deportees vanished through the giant doors, after a while we found ourselves closer to the railings, with a good view of the whole operation, the old man was still standing there

Hey, he's waving at us, Namredef shouted at me, I swear he is, and for a few moments both of us waved back at the old man, I even took out my handkerchief from my pocket and waved it deliriously, but he was not really waving, no, we finally decided, he had simply raised his hand either to scratch his head or swat away a pesty fly, it was hard to tell from where we stood, and anyway the old man wasn't looking in our direction, but toward the spaceship, just then someone stepped on my toes, I cursed the fellow and bent down to wipe my shoe, and there, on the floor, I saw a graffito

A graffito, what do you mean, can you explain that

Yes a graffito scratched on the seamless floor, I was so aston-ished I pulled at Namredef's sleeve and motioned him to look down, we both got down on our hands and knees, literally, to try and decipher the meaning of this curious inscription, it had been trampled by so many feet it was almost invisible, but as we wiped it with our hands and with my handkerchief, we gra-dually discovered that someone had carved, rather clumsily but not without style, five playing cards, you know, gambling cards, the ten, the jack, the queen, the king, the ace, all in spades, in that order from left to right, and above this royal flush, this second perfect royal flush that came our way by pure chance, were scribbled the words Temporarily Saved, at least that's what I thought it said, but Namredef argued with me that it really said Temporarily Sane, quite a different meaning, don't you think

I don't know how you can arrive at a four-letter word like that, I told him, from what is definitely a five-letter scribbling, but the argument was interrupted when I heard Namredef shout at someone, Hey will you get the fuck off my hand, and a fat man, I mean really huge, 250, 300 pounds, lifted his pachydermous foot and apologized as Namredef held his right hand in his left obviously in pain, it did hurt, didn't it Nam, Damn right it was hurting

What the hell are you two jerks doing down there, the fat man asked shaking his head in disgust, playing games

we didn't answer, we got up and turned away from him, somewhat embarrassed, but still puzzled by the graffito which didn't seem to mean anything to us, though perhaps it was a sign, even the answer to the whole situation, but we couldn't understand it, meanwhile next to us two other persons were also on their hands and knees trying to decipher another in-scription, we even heard them argue in a whisper, No I tell you, it says Free Village, one of them was saying, but the other insisted, You're wrong, it says Free the Village, quite a differ-

ent meaning, we were tempted to get involved in this interesting discussion which may also have had something to do with
the present situation, but it dawned on us that this series of little
incidents, these foolish distractions had made us lose sight of
the old man

we looked around, I don't see him anywhere, did they call his
name already, I asked Namredef

No they couldn't have, I didn't hear it, he replied, trying to
hide the anxiety in his voice

the lines of departees had perceptibly thinned and still there
was no sign of the old man, we started calling his name in
unison, even though it might draw attention to us, we were
desperate, the situation was getting ridiculous

Why don't I stand on your shoulders to look for him, I told
Namredef after we were both hoarse from shouting

Why can't I stand on yours, he countered, I am always the one
who has to support you

That's not true, I said, but look let's not start another futile
argument, let's just flip a coin to decide

Namredef agreed, our first three coins were lost in the crowd
under heavy feet, but finally I won, heads it was, I climbed on
Namredef's shoulders, but not without some stumbling and
grumbling, Nam was staggering so dangerously when I managed to stand on his shoulders that I thought for sure the two of
us would crash to the ground, but somehow he succeeded in
planting his feet squarely and held on firmly to my ankles, I
cuffed my eyes with my hand like an old sailor and searched for
the old man among the groups of deportees who were still
standing in front of the doors, he was not to be seen anywhere,
Hey Nam I think this time we really goofed, I said still perched
precariously on his shoulders, we missed the most important
moment, do you realize what a stupid thing we did, after all

this, to come that far and miss the most crucial moment, I feel terrible, terrible, don't you

What do you think, Namredef answered, of course I feel shitty, but admit it was all your fault with that fucking graffito

Here you go again, always blaming me, but then suddenly I saw him, There he is, I cried, I see him, that old fart, over there, over there on the right

the old man was just rising from the floor as though he too had been on his hands and knees doing something down there, I don't know what, for sure not praying, not him

Maybe he was also trying to decipher a graffito, I suggest, from what you guys are saying, the floor seemed to be full of graffiti, or else he was simply tying up his shoelaces

No, Namredef corrects me, not his shoelaces because the deportees were wearing sandals

Okay then, fixing his sandals, what's the difference, I was just guessing, I say relieved to hear that they had found the old man, So what happened after that

By now the hall was more than half empty, from both ends, both sides of the railings, most of the deportees had moved out to the embarkation platform and the visitors connected with these had departed, we were in the front row now, the loudspeakers were still calling out names in a monotone, but our old man still stood there in the middle of a few hundred or so white tunics

then only a few dozens were left, at this point Namredef and I started counting how many deportees were left, 35, 34, 33, 32, it was like a countdown, 16, 15, 14, less than a dozen now, 9, 8, 7, and finally the old man stood alone

strange, we looked around, and we were the only two visitors left, we had no idea what the hell was going on, a few attendants had gathered together, but far away in a corner of the great hall, and they didn't seem to be paying attention to the old man or to us, you can't imagine the feeling of emptiness in that hall

Attention, Attention, the loudspeakers blared, Clear the area, all personnel must leave the hall of departure immediately, countdown has begun, clear the area immediately, five minutes to launching, and slowly the great doors slid shut with a thunderous clang that resounded deafeningly around the hall, we looked at each other, frozen in our place by the railings, the emptiness of the hall and the silence which settled in after the echo faded away were almost unbearable, What's going on, I asked Namredef, why didn't they call his name, How would I know, he replied shrugging his shoulders in a gesture of total bafflement, but there was deep anguish in his voice

we couldn't understand why the old man was still standing there and no one seemed to be concerned, we thought of calling out to him but decided not to draw attention to our presence, especially now, it was so quiet in that hall, frighteningly quiet, and so empty, can you imagine that immense space totally empty, except for the three of us, I mean Nam and I behind the railings, and the old man all alone, hundreds of yards away in the middle of the floor, we must have looked like ants seen from above, a cough, a whisper, a sneeze would have echoed and carried throughout that hall like noises in a Greek amphitheater, we didn't know what to do, where to go, and so we waited

even the attendants had disappeared, then suddenly the old man let out a scream toward the loudspeakers, a scream louder perhaps than he intended because the hall filled and reverberated with the sound of his voice, BUT WHAT ABOUT ME, WHAT ABOUT ME, he cried several times as he struck his chest with his hands

for the first time since he had been at the spaceport we heard despair in his voice, What about me, he repeated again, the sound of his voice becoming fainter and fainter as he kept repeating that phrase, but his question was met with silence, a silence as long and empty as the hall itself, then out of a little door on the far end of the hall an electric cart sped toward us

we were told to leave immediately

But, but Sir, we tried to say to the man in the buggy, pointing to the solitary figure in the middle of the hall

Gentlemen you must leave this place at once, we were told politely but firmly, Everything will be taking care of, and so we left, in the electric cart in fact as the attendant drove us to the exit and out of the building, after that we came here directly

That's it, I say, that's the whole story, you mean to say you don't even know what happened to the old man, where he went, what they did with him, after all that, after all we've gone through, the days, weeks, months of probing, questioning, worrying, agonizing over the old man's fate, that's all you have to say, I look at Namredef and Moinous, they are still sitting on the sofa in my study, I cannot tell if it is fear or happiness I see in their eyes

Yes, that's all we saw, that's all we heard, these were his last words, But what about me, and nobody answered, and as they speak these words Namredef and Moinous get up from the sofa, put on their coats, Well that's all we have to report, they say, then they shake hands with me and leave, just like that, without another word

confused, disgusted, crushed, I sit at my desk, head between my hands, and stare at the blank sheet of paper in front of me, what do I do now, can I go on, and where to, and for what purpose

I close my eyes, Namredef and Moinous fade away into my subconscious, I feel empty, useless, then suddenly I murmur to myself, If the night passes quietly tomorrow

hours pass, I must have dozed off, it's still dark outside, a barrage of unresolved events confronts me, I shiver, it is cold, what now, then I remember the words I scribbled, so long ago when I first thought of this project, those enigmatic words which kept circling in my head, But the persistence of the twofold vibration suggests that in this old abode all is not yet quite for the best, and sure enough, now I understand, I understand, there is nothing else to do

I close my eyes again

Well, goodnight you guys, you can go back to sleep now